The troop crested a rise in the ground and the soldiers saw the cause of the smoke. A half mile ahead lay what was left of a wagon train. Black, charred wood, twisted iron and steel, shreds of scorched canvas and a number of huddled bodies. They found the embers still warm to the touch, the wagon tires hot. The bodies still had the blood, uncongealed. There were nineteen, including three women and two children. All had been scalped, most of them mutilated.

"The bloody heathens," one trooper swore softly. Another said, "I still say Sheridan's got the right idea. Kill every goddamn Indian in the West and you'll get peace. They're savages and that's the way we ought to treat them."

Ⓢ A Signet Brand Western

SIGNET Westerns For Your Enjoyment

- ☐ **BITTER SAGE** by Frank Gruber. (#W8963—$1.50)
- ☐ **QUANTRELL'S RAIDERS** by Frank Gruber. (#J9735—$1.95)
- ☐ **RETURN OF A FIGHTER** by Ernest Haycox. (#E9419—$1.75)
- ☐ **RIDERS WEST** by Ernest Haycox. (#J9979—$1.95)
- ☐ **SUNDOWN JIM** by Ernest Haycox. (#E9796—$1.75)
- ☐ **TRAIL TOWN** by Ernest Haycox. (#J9779—$1.95)
- ☐ **THE DOOMSDAY TRAIL** by Ray Hogan. (#E9354—$1.75)
- ☐ **THE HELL RAISER** by Ray Hogan. (#E9489—$1.75)
- ☐ **OUTLAW'S PLEDGE** by Ray Hogan. (#J9778—$1.95)
- ☐ **PILGRIM** by Ray Hogan. (#E9576—$1.75)
- ☐ **THE RAPTORS** by Ray Hogan. (#E9124—$1.75)
- ☐ **THE DEAD GUN** by Ray Hogan. (#E9026—$1.75)
- ☐ **THE ANGRY HORSEMEN** by Lewis B. Patten. (#E9309—$1.75)
- ☐ **POSSE FROM POISON CREEK** by Lewis B. Patten. (#E9577—$1.75)
- ☐ **PURSUIT** by Lewis B. Patten. (#E9209—$1.75)

Buy them at your local bookstore or use this convenient coupon for ordering.

THE NEW AMERICAN LIBRARY, INC.,
P.O. Box 999, Bergenfield, New Jersey 07621

Please send me the books I have checked above. I am enclosing $_____
(please add $1.00 to this order to cover postage and handling). Send check
or money order—no cash or C.O.D.'s. Prices and numbers are subject to change
without notice.

Name_____

Address_____

City _____ State _____ Zip Code _____
Allow 4-6 weeks for delivery.
This offer is subject to withdrawal without notice.

Broken Lance

by FRANK GRUBER

A SIGNET BOOK

NEW AMERICAN LIBRARY

TIMES MIRROR

NAL BOOKS ARE AVAILABLE AT QUANTITY DISCOUNTS
WHEN USED TO PROMOTE PRODUCTS OR SERVICES. FOR
INFORMATION PLEASE WRITE TO PREMIUM MARKETING
DIVISION, THE NEW AMERICAN LIBRARY, INC., 1633
BROADWAY, NEW YORK, NEW YORK 10019.

COPYRIGHT, 1948, 1949, BY FRANK GRUBER
COPYRIGHT © RENEWED 1976, 1977 BY LOIS GRUBER

All rights reserved. For information address Mrs. Lois Gruber
c/o The New American Library, Inc., 1633 Broadway,
New York, New York 10019.

Published by arrangement with Mrs. Lois Gruber

SIGNET TRADEMARK REG. U.S. PAT. OFF. AND FOREIGN COUNTRIES
REGISTERED TRADEMARK—MARCA REGISTRADA
HECHO EN CHICAGO, U.S.A.

SIGNET, SIGNET CLASSICS, MENTOR, PLUME, MERIDIAN AND NAL
BOOKS are published by The New American Library, Inc.,
1633 Broadway, New York, New York 10019

FIRST SIGNET PRINTING, AUGUST, 1976

3 4 5 6 7 8 9 10 11

PRINTED IN THE UNITED STATES OF AMERICA

Broken Lance

One

THE tramp sat on the high wooden sidewalk, his feet kicking the dust of Canal Street. He was an unusually disreputable-looking man, his face covered with a two-weeks' growth of beard, his clothes in tatters. A floppy, shapeless hat with part of the brim torn off was perched on top of a head that had needed a haircut months ago.

A horsecar stopped on Madison Street, some fifty feet from where the tramp sat. A passenger catapulted from the car, landing on his hands and feet. The conductor and a couple of male passengers swarmed out and leaped upon the first man while he was still sprawled on the ground. For a moment there was a furious scuffle, then one of the men screamed in sudden anguish and fell back. The first man tore loose from his assailants and started running up Canal Street. There was a long-bladed jackknife in his fist, from which blood dripped.

The conductor of the horsecar stared after the fugitive, yelling at the top of his lungs: "Stop that man! He's a pickpocket and murderer!"

The fleeing man came pelting down Canal Street, heading for the east side of the street and the railroad tracks beyond. The tramp, still seated on the wooden sidewalk, watched his approach with indifference. For a moment. Then, suddenly he sprang to his feet.

"Herb Woodley!" he gasped in complete astonishment.

The fugitive shot a startled glance over his shoulder, then his legs seemed to churn the dust even faster. For a moment the tramp stood as if rooted to the ground, then a shudder ran through his lean body and he darted after the man he had identified as Herb Woodley.

He had only a few feet head start on the conductor and the passengers from the horsecar, but he ran so swiftly that he quickly outdistanced them.

The fleeing man was perhaps forty feet ahead of the

3

tramp. Reaching the far sidewalk, he darted into a passage way between two stores. At the end of the passageway was a high wooden fence. Woodley skidded to a halt in front of it. He whirled, threw the knife at the tramp, his closest pursuer, and thrust his hand into a pocket.

"Keep back!" he cried hoarsely. A gun appeared in his fist.

The tramp came to an abrupt stop. "Put that gun away," he ordered.

Behind the tramp, the other pursuers pounded into the passageway. There were exclamations of alarm and chagrin, as they saw the gun in the hand of Woodley.

Woodley looked at the height of the fence, groaned and then thrust the gun again in the direction of the tramp and the men behind him.

"Get back!" he yelled. "Get back, or I'll shoot."

"Shoot," the tramp said, hoarsely, "shoot and be damned to you, Herb Woodley."

For an instant Woodley stood his ground and it seemed that he was going to shoot, but then more people came up behind the tramp and he decided that his only chance stood in getting over the fence. He thrust the gun into his pocket and sprang for the top of the fence. He caught hold of it with both hands, pulled himself up and threw one foot over the top.

The tramp sprang forward. Woodley, hearing the clatter of his feet on the boardwalk, twisted around and saw the tramp charging for the fence. He exclaimed in alarm and again reached for the gun that he had jammed into his pocket. The movement caused him to lose his balance on the top of the fence. He clawed wildly to recover, but could not quite make it and fell on the far side. He had scarcely struck the ground than the tramp was taking the fence.

Woodley clambered to his feet, only to have his ankle turn under him. He cried out in pain and fell to his hands and knees as the tramp hit the ground beside him.

The gun had fallen from Woodley's hand and lay a yard from him. Seeing his peril he lunged for it. But the tramp beat him to it. He got his hand on it and started to whirl. Woodley, in desperation, kicked at him with his uninjured foot, upsetting the tramp.

He fell on his side and Woodley, drawing himself together, started to pounce on him. The tramp threw himself on his back; the gun in his hand came up and belched fire and thunder.

Woodley cried out in anguish, rose to his feet. Clutching at his chest he swayed for a moment, then fell backwards to the ground.

There was a babel of voices on the other side of the fence, a sudden scurrying of feet.

The tramp scrambled to his feet, stepped up to Woodley and looked down. The pickpocket was still clutching his chest. Blood seeped through his fingers and a trickle of red was dribbling from his mouth. His eyes were twisted in agony. He was dying.

"Woodley," said the tramp, through clenched teeth, "I'm John Leach . . ."

The dying man's eyes were forced open. An expression of amazement and horror came into them. "Leach," he croaked, "you've been hounding me for years. Everywhere I've gone you've been on my trail. What—what kind of a man are you?"

The man called Leach said harshly: "I've followed you for eight years. I swore I'd get you and—"

He broke off as a fit of choking racked Woodley. Blood welled up into his mouth, gushed forth in a torrent. Leach, stooping, caught hold of the dying man's coat front. He shook Woodley.

"You're dying, Woodley," he cried. "In a minute you'll be facing your maker . . ."

"Damn you . . . Leach," choked Woodley. "Damn you . . ." Then a spasm of pain stopped him.

The face of a man appeared over the top of the fence, remained suspended as he looked down upon the tableau below. Leach, heedless, continued to belabor the dying Woodley.

"Woodley, where are Morrison and Bligh? Tell me before you die."

"Go . . . to . . . hell . . . !"

A groan of frustration escaped Leach's lips. He let go

of Woodley and the dying man's head fell back to the ground.

A second head appeared above the top of the fence. Legs followed and a man dropped to the ground. Another man clambered over, then others.

Leach's eyes never left those of the man on the ground. Life was ebbing swiftly from Woodley's tortured body. A slow sigh escaped his lips and Leach, stooping again, thought the man dead. But then the lips parted once more.

"Joined . . ." came from the bloodied lips. "Joined . . . the . . . Cav . . . alry . . ."

A bubble of blood formed on the lips, broke, and Woodley was dead.

Leach stared down for a moment, then became aware that he was still holding the dead man's gun. He hurled it to the ground.

Beside Leach, a man said hoarsely: "He's dead!"

"Yes, he's dead," Leach said bitterly. "But he died too quickly. He didn't . . . suffer . . ."

The man stared at Leach in awe.

Two

PASSENGERS were dropping from the steps of the rickety wooden coaches even before the train came to a halt. There would be only a half-hour's stop here; the lunchroom was a small one and the train had a full complement of westbound passengers.

They poured into the eating room, weatherbeaten farmers of the Dakota plains, prospectors headed for the Black Hills, cattlemen, soldiers, women, young and old. Even an Indian or two.

John Leach was one of the last to leave the train and when he reached the door of the lunchroom he saw that all the seats at the counters inside were filled and that quite a number of people were already waiting. His breakfast had been skimpy and the thought of going without food until evening did not please him. He opened the screen door and entered the restaurant.

A quick glance at the nearest counter raised Leach's hopes. There were beans in front of every place, underdone, hard-looking beans. The diners would eat quickly and sparingly. Even as Leach thought of it, a man pushed back his plate, scarcely touched. He dropped a dollar on the counter and got off his stool.

"I wouldn't feed my pigs such slops," he said in disgust and turned away.

A girl in a green velvet traveling suit moved up to take the vacated stool. At the same time a blue-uniformed soldier with sergeant's chevrons on his sleeve stepped forward from the other side. He beat the girl to the seat, placed his hand upon it and smirked, "The Army's beat you, lady," he said, "but I don't mind selling you this place for a small price. Say, a kiss."

The girl gave him a withering glance and stepped back. A second soldier, a corporal, moved up behind the sergeant and guffawed. "The lady'd rather not eat, Sergeant."

The sergeant's face, already red from drinking, got even darker. "I've kissed better'n her in honky-tonks," he snapped. He stepped away from the lunch counter stool and made a sudden lunge for the girl.

He would have gotten his hands on her, except that Leach lurched forward and the sergeant collided with him.

"Get outta my way," the sergeant snarled. He shoved roughly on Leach but found his body hard and unyielding.

"Easy does it, Sergeant," Leach said smoothly.

The sergeant stared at Leach in astonishment. "Are you trying to pick a fight with me?" he cried. " 'Cause if you are, you've—" He broke off and sent a sizzling blow at Leach's head, which the latter ducked easily.

Leach stepped away. "You're drunk, soldier."

The sergeant's shoulders came up and made him look even bigger than he was. "Drunk or sober," he said thickly, "I don't take that from any man."

A sudden silence had fallen upon the eating room. It was broken by the girl in the green suit. "Please," she said. "I'd just as soon not eat."

It was a ridiculous statement to make at this stage of the game and neither Leach or the sergeant paid any attention to it.

His eyes fixed upon the baleful eyes of the soldier. Leach reached sidewards and pushed open the door of the lunchroom. He backed out and was followed closely by the sergeant. On the station platform Leach continued to back away.

The soldier, mistaking Leach's desire for plenty of room, sneered: "You wanted a fight, stand still and take your beating."

The two men were of a same height, six feet, within a fraction, but Leach weighed one hundred and seventy pounds and the other man at least thirty more. Leach's shabby clothes and his two days' growth of beard gave him a deceptively drawn appearance, but his body was solid bone and muscle.

He stopped his retreat. "All right, Sergeant," he said, "make your fight."

A cruel grin twisted the red face of the sergeant. He stepped forward, made a sudden feint with his left fist and swung savagely with his right. Had the blow landed, the fight would have ended then and there. But Leach ducked smoothly under the swishing fist and struck a light blow into the soldier's midriff.

The sergeant grunted. "If that's all you've got, mister," he snorted, "you're a dead duck right now."

He stepped forward contemptuously and swung a roundhouse right. Leach took the blow on his shoulder and let it swing him to the rear and right. From that position he uncorked a right hook that exploded on the soldier's jaw. He followed with a smashing blow to the stomach, another right to the jaw and then a left into the bigger man's face. Blood splattered his fist and the sergeant, gasping, fell back.

Leach followed him, became a bit too confident and staggered back from a tremendous blow on his chest. The sergeant, bellowing, charged him like a wild bull, both fists flailing.

Leach realized that he had underestimated the big man. Liquored he was, but he had lived a rough, outdoor life. Those two hundred odd pounds were solid. The man could take plenty and could deal it out, too.

Gritting his teeth, Leach went in a crouch. A fist grazed the side of his head, another crashed against his raised left arm, almost numbing it. Then Leach moved forward. He swung his right into the bigger man's midriff, drove in his left with every ounce of strength in his body, then, straightening, smashed the sergeant's face with a right and left. The soldier fell back, panting hoarsely. He was still swinging wildly, but the power had gone from him. Leach took a blow that scarcely hurt.

And suddenly Leach stepped back. Measuring the sergeant, he put everything he had into one final blow that hit the sergeant in the jaw and toppled him over backwards onto the wooden station platform.

The soldier landed with a crash. He was still conscious but unable to regain his feet. The corporal who had been with him in the lunchroom sprang foward and dropped to his knees beside his comrade-in-arms.

He saw that his friend was only momentarily incapacitated and bounced to his feet. "All right," he snarled at Leach, "you got me to lick now."

"No," said Leach, "I've no fight with you."

"The devil you haven't," cried the corporal and leaped at Leach. He was a wiry little man, not more than one hundred and fifty pounds in weight and standing around five feet seven. But his fist smacked Leach high in the face and stung. Groaning, Leach hit the little man a savage blow in the stomach that sent him reeling back.

The corporal would have returned to the fight, but at that moment, the sergeant gained a sitting position and the corporal deemed that assistance to his friend had first claim upon him. He turned, helped the sergeant to his feet.

"Can you make it, Denny?" he asked anxiously.

The sergeant brushed the little corporal aside. "Where is he?" he asked thickly. "I'll murder him."

"Here I am," said Leach soberly.

Around them passengers were hurrying from the lunchroom back to the train. The conductor's voice rose above the clatter and bustle. " 'Bo-oard . . . !"

Relieved, Leach rushed past the two soldiers for the train. He deliberately went past his former coach and clambered aboard the one behind it. He found a seat by a window and dropped heavily into it. After a moment, as the train started moving, he drew a soiled handkerchief from his pocket and dabbed at his cheekbone, where he felt a warm trickle of blood.

Someone sat down beside him, but Leach did not look. A calm voice said:

"Thank you."

Leach's head swiveled and he looked into the face of the girl in the green velvet dress.

"Oh," he said. "You . . ."

She held up a tissue-wrapped package. "I brought you a sandwich, since I was the cause of you missing your lunch."

Leach grinned crookedly. "I don't think you had a chance to eat yourself."

10

"There are two sandwiches in here," she said, calmly, and began unwrapping them.

Leach stowed away his handkerchief, hesitated, then took one of the sandwiches from her. He took a bite of it, winced a little.

"I think he loosened a tooth."

"From the looks of him as I passed, he's got more than a loose tooth," the girl said. She looked at him thoughtfully. "I was afraid at first that you'd tackled a bit too much."

Leach shrugged. "I was in the car ahead all morning. I saw him put away at least a pint of whiskey. A man can't fight his best with that much in him."

The girl munched at her sandwich. Leach ate his own and finishing, said: "You're going to Bismarck?"

She nodded. "Yes. It isn't much of a town, is it?"

"I've never been there. But it's the end of the railroad and has Fort Lincoln, so I imagine it's a pretty rough place."

"So Dad wrote me. He's at the fort."

Leach gave her a quick glance. "An officer?"

"No, a sutler." She smiled. "By the way, my name is Molly Quade."

"How do you do, Molly Quade," Leach said softly. "I imagine I'll be seeing you at the fort. I'm going there to enlist."

She looked at him in surprise. "You're traveling to Bismarck deliberately to enlist in the Army?"

"In the Seventh Cavalry."

A little frown creased her forehead. "You'll be an enlisted man, a private . . ." She did not finish the sentence, but her eyes went to the door of the coach.

Leach expressed the thought in her mind. "And I've just got through fighting with a sergeant in the Seventh."

"Well," she said, "I hope you don't wind up in his troop, under him."

"The odds are against it."

11

Three

BISMARCK was a shabby little town of a single street of false-fronted buildings. But the activity on the street belied the smallness of the place. Bismarck was the end of the railroad, the gateway to the Black Hills. It was a farmer's town, cattleman's headquarters, Army post and jumping-off place, all in one.

A man with a Ulysses S. Grant beard was on the station platform as Molly Quade descended from the day coach steps. He took her into his arms, and Leach, coming down the steps behind Molly, seized the opportunity to melt into the throng on the depot platform.

A short distance from the depot Leach stopped a man.

"How do I get out to the fort?"

"Which fort?"

"I thought Fort Lincoln was the only fort around this neighborhood."

"Well, it is and she's the biggest doggone fort this side of St. Paul. Mmm, you've got yourself a right smart walk if you expect to get out there before sundown. Four mile and then you cross the river on the ferry—"

"Thank you," said Leach patiently, "now if you'll tell me in which direction to do that walking . . ."

"Why walk when you can ride?" asked the loquacious citizen of Bismarck. He pointed to an Army ambulance. "There's a bus goin' right out to the fort. They'll give you a lift, I'm sure. The driver's—"

"Thanks," cut in Leach, already moving toward the Army ambulance.

A couple of soldiers were just climbing aboard the wagon. One of them was the sergeant whom Leach had fought at the lunch station stop on the railroad; the other was his corporal friend. The sergeant had a mouse on his left cheekbone and his right eye was completely closed. He scowled at Leach with his unwounded eye.

"What the devil do *you* want here?" he snapped.

"A ride to the fort," Leach said calmly.

"This wagon belongs to the Army," retorted the sergeant.

"Of which I hope to be a member in about an hour," Leach said. "I'm going out to the fort to enlist."

The sergeant stared at him in astonishment. "You want to—to enlist?"

"Why not?" Leach asked cheerfully. "I'm told that Army life's good for a man."

"Jeez," said the stocky corporal, "I hope I get you in my troop. I'll learn you a thing or two."

"As to that, Shorty," said Leach, "I'll be trying for some stripes myself."

The corporal sneered. "It took me six years to get these. Stripes come hard in the Seventh. You've got to *earn* them."

"Good," said Leach, nodding. He looked at the sergeant. "Do I get the ride?"

"You get it," the sergeant gritted, "and in a day or two when I sweat the booze out of my system, I'll be lookin' you up."

"That's your privilege."

Leach climbed into the ambulance and two privates who had been standing near by followed. One turned out to be the driver of the ambulance and, taking up the lines, he cracked the whip over a handsome team of bays.

The ambulance rolled swiftly out of Bismarck and followed a winding road that led along the river. In a half hour or so the ambulance boarded a flat-bottomed scow that deposited them across the river where it climbed a steep grade and entered Fort Abraham Lincoln.

It was a massive enclosure, ideally situated and built to withstand the attacks of any possible Indian hordes. The back sides of the barracks, stables, storehouses and other necessary buildings, formed the outer wall and in the center was a great parade ground, large enough for cavalry drills.

The sergeant tapped the driver on the shoulder shortly after the ambulance had entered the fort. "Stop here," he ordered.

13

The ambulance came to a halt and the sergeant nodded to Leach. "Headquarters, where you enlist . . . if they'll have you." He strode off, entering the headquarters building, as Leach got down from the ambulance.

"Stockbridge is my name," the little corporal told him, then. "Corporal Stockbridge of Troop M. I'll be seeing you around, I hope."

"Good enough." Leach started to turn away, then wheeled back. "What's the sergeant's name?"

"Dennis O'Hara, what else? And he's senior line sergeant of Troop M, the best troop in the whole regiment."

Leach nodded and crossed to the headquarters building. He stopped for a moment, then drawing a deep breath, entered. A headquarters clerk with corporal's chevrons on his sleeve sat at a plain wooden table, talking to Sergeant O'Hara.

"Who do I see about enlisting?" Leach asked.

"Me," replied the corporal. "Me and Major Comstock."

Sergeant O'Hara, grinning wickedly at Leach, winked at the corporal and left the room. The corporal pulled out a drawer in the table, brought out an enlistment blank and picking up a pen, looked at Leach.

"If you'll give me your name and the vital statistics . . . ?"

"Name, John Leach."

"Place of birth?"

"Lexington, Missouri."

"A Johnny Reb, eh?"

"Hardly."

The corporal grunted. "Age?"

"Thirty-one."

"Previous service, if any?"

"Troop G. Thirty-second Missouri, Mounted," Leach answered quietly.

The corporal looked up at him in some surprise.

"During the Big Fight?"

"April, 1861, to July, 1865."

"The full treatment, eh? Rank at date of discharge? If any."

14

Leach hesitated. "Brevet captain."

The corporal put down his pen. "A captain! Well!"

A man wearing the shoulder straps of a major entered the room from a side door. The corporal caught up his pen again. "Uh, Major Comstock, sir, this man wants to enlist. He's, ah, a former captain."

Major Comstock came forward, looked sharply into Leach's face, then dropped his eyes to his shabby attire. "What outfit?"

"Thirty-second Missouri, sir."

The major grunted. "The Thirty-Second did a rather good job Yellow Tavern. Mmm, you commanded Troop G, did you not?"

"Yes, sir."

"I thought I recognized you."

"Yes, sir, you commanded the third brigade at the time."

"That's right." A slight frown creased the major's forehead. "You know, of course, that The General is commanding this regiment?"

"Yes, sir."

"And you're aware that the Seventh is considered a crack regiment? You know what makes a crack regiment, in peacetime."

"Drill, sir."

"And discipline."

"Yes, sir."

The frown was still on the major's face. "I was thinking, well, that a former officer might find such a routine a bit, shall we say, distasteful?"

"I don't mind drill, sir. And discipline."

The major hesitated, then suddenly turned on the corporal. "Enlist this man, Corporal."

"Very good, sir."

Major Comstock pursed up his lips, regarded Leach for a moment, then nodded, stepped past him, and strode out of the room to the parade ground.

The corporal finished scribbling on the enlistment blank then looked up sidewards at Leach. "Know Longhair?"

"Lieutenant Colonel Custer?"

15

"He still likes to be called General."

Leach made no reply to that and the corporal stood up. "Come next door with me and we'll have the doc look you over. If you pass, I guess you can be sworn in."

The corporal led the way outside and to a door next to Headquarters, where a lieutenant in the medical corps was seated at a desk.

"Lieutenant," the corporal said, "Major Comstock would appreciate if you'd examine this man at once, with a view to his enlisting in the Seventh."

The lieutenant nodded. "Very well, if you'll strip."

The corporal left Leach with the medical officer and Leach peeled off his clothing. The lieutenant tapped him here and there, looked into his mouth and listened to his heart and after a few minutes nodded approval. "You'll do."

Leach began donning his clothes and, before he had finished, Major Comstock entered.

"All right?" he asked.

"Good enough for any Indian," the lieutenant responded, cheerfully.

"Ready to be sworn in then, Leach?" asked the major. "This is your last chance to back out."

"I came here all the way from Chicago for only one purpose," Leach said, "to enlist in the Seventh Cavalry."

"Very well, then raise your right hand."

One minute later, Major Comstock held out his hand. "You're now a trooper in the Seventh Cavalry."

Leach shook hands with the major, then came to attention.

"Yes, sir."

"Report back to the office next door, and you'll be assigned. The corporal has a list of the troop vacancies."

Leach hesitated a moment, then saluted smartly. About-facing, he left the room.

In the next room, the corporal was awaiting him. "The last recruit went to Troop J," he said, "but M's about as short of men as any, so—"

"Troop M," said Leach, "Sergeant O'Hara's troop."

"Why, yes, I believe O'Hara's in Troop M. Why . . . ?"

"I thought he might have asked for me."

"So he did. Friend, isn't he?"

"No."

The corporal chuckled. "Of course if you want to go over my head . . ."

"Would it do any good?"

"Since the major's an old buddy of yours, probably yes. And if he says no, you can go over *his* head, right up to Longhair himself."

"I'll take Troop M."

"Sure enough? Well, that's mighty sociable of you, Private. Here's your papers. You'll find Troop M right smack across the parade ground. If First Sergeant Parker's sitting in a poker game, Sergeant O'Hara will take care of you, I'm sure."

Four

LEACH accepted his enlistment records and, leaving the headquarters office, crossed the parade grounds to the long row of barracks beyond. The barracks of Troop M were identified by a sign and he entered the orderly room.

The company clerk took his papers, examined them and looked sharply at Leach. "Just a minute," he said. He stepped through a door and Leach heard the rumbling of voices for a moment. Then the clerk returned with the first sergeant, a lean man with greying hair.

He came toward Leach. "I'm Parker, top kick. This is an interesting service record you have."

Leach merely nodded. The sergeant cleared his throat. "Captain Holterman's the skipper here. Know him?"

"No, I don't."

"Thought you might. He had a regiment under Pleasanton. But come to think of it he went out to Missouri when Pleasanton was shifted there." He paused. "A good man, the skipper. Fair. I'll show him your service record."

"No need for that."

"Eh?"

"I'm not looking for a promotion—if that's what you had in mind."

The first sergeant frowned down at the service records in his hand. "You didn't by any chance have a, well, a bit of trouble on the outside?"

"The law isn't looking for me."

"Good. Not that it would make any difference. We don't give a damn what a man's done before he enlisted. Not unless it affects him here." First Sergeant Parker made a slight gesture. "Look up the supply sergeant and get your equipment. And you might see if the cook'll give you something to eat. You missed chow."

Leach found the supply sergeant's quarters at the rear

18

of the barracks and there was issued uniforms, blankets, a few toilet articles and a carbine. Before he was ready, the company clerk sought him out.

"I've assigned you to Squad Room A," he said. "Corporal Stockbridge will show you your bunk."

In Squad Room A, which overlooked the parade ground, Corporal Stockbridge chuckled wickedly when Leach made his appearance. "Well, well, me bucko, and here we are!" He clapped Leach on the shoulder, using a little more force than was necessary. "I'll have to take good care of you. Let's see, now, there's a vacant cot right there between Limey and Fiore. Private Egan used to have it, him that died of gallopin' pneumonia only last week."

Leach dumped his equipment on the designated cot. A long-legged, sandy-haired soldier sprawled on the cot to the right, winked at him.

"The corporal's a great one for jokes," he said.

"Speaking of jokes," Stockbridge said, baring his teeth, "when was you on kitchen police last, Limey?"

"Yesterday," replied the soldier called Limey. "And I had latrine duty the day before."

"Is that so? I remember now, you did a mighty fine job with those latrines. I think I'll recommend you for the duty again in a day or two."

"You do that, Corporal," retorted Limey. "And maybe some night we'll be seeing each other at The Point."

"Is that a threat, Limey?"

"A threat, Corporal? Me, make a threat to a superior? Me, who's been a soldier in one Army or another for fourteen years?"

The corporal scowled and went off. Limey sat up on his cot and held out his hand to Leach. "Potts, Cecil Potts, late of Her Majesty's Indian Rifles, also Garibaldi's Carabiniers."

"You've been around," said Leach, shaking the Englishman's hand.

Potts grinned. "Also, a hitch with Price's Robbers, of Missouri."

"Confederate!"

The Englishman shrugged. "An error of judgment. I

19

thought the South would win. However, I switched over to the Yanks in '64. Just in time."

Leach found an empty locker behind his cot and began stowing away his gear. The Englishman watched him until Leach was clad in his new blue uniform.

"Makes a difference, doesn't it?"

Leach nodded. "What sort of a lad is this Sergeant O'Hara?"

Potts grimaced. "An Orangeman, no less. He's licked every man in the troop at least once and he's working on the second round now. A bad one." He screwed up his lips. "A fair soldier, though."

Leach started to make up his bed. "Ever hear of a soldier named Bligh?"

"In Troop M?"

"I thought he might be in one of the other troops."

"Never heard the name, but then there are a thousand soldiers at Fort Lincoln. Friend?"

"Not exactly." Leach sat down on the cot. "What about Morrison?"

"Charlie Morrison? Top Sergeant of L Troop. Old-timer."

"How old?"

"He's got four hash marks on his sleeve."

Leach creased his forehead in thought. "He wouldn't be over thirty-five, or thirty-seven."

"No. Sergeant Morrison's fifty, probably more."

"Then I guess it isn't the same man."

A heavy step sounded just outside the squad room and Sergeant O'Hara made his appearance. "Ah, Private, you've put on your brand new uniform. Good. Good. Got a little job for you."

It was beginning. Leach got to his feet. "Yes?"

"If you'll be so good as to follow me . . ."

"A little latrine duty, Sarge?" asked Trooper Potts.

"I'll get around to you later," O'Hara promised. "Come on, Leach."

He started out of the squad room, Leach following. Outside, O'Hara led the way to a long, shedlike building at the far end of the parade ground. As they approached,

Leach's nostrils caught the strong odor of horses and realized what was before him.

O'Hara opened the stable door and waited for Leach to enter. He pointed to a section of horses, each in its individual stall. "This place is a mess," he declared. "Somebody's going to catch it tomorrow, but in the meantime you can do a spot of cleaning here."

"And after I finish?"

"You can hit the hay." O'Hara smiled thinly. "Remember now, only the stalls belonging to M Troop. I think there's seventy-two. It shouldn't take you over three or four hours, at the most. But do a good job."

Leach found a fork and broom and pitched into the work. O'Hara watched him for a few minutes, perhaps hoping for a protest from Leach, but got none and left the stables.

A grizzled old soldier, in fatigues, wandered up after awhile. "How come?" he asked.

"I'm a recruit. Sergeant O'Hara's breaking me in properly."

"In the old dragoons, every man took care of his own horse," the old-timer said.

"But even in the old Army, noncoms rode men, didn't they?" Leach asked.

"Oh, it's like that, eh? Well, I've heard that O'Hara's as mean as a Pawnee. Got it in for you, has he?"

"A little. But I can stand it." Leach leaned on his manure fork. "Been in quite a spell?"

"Since '49. Four years more and they put me out to grass."

"How long have you been in the Seventh?"

"Since it was organized in '66. Fort Riley, first."

"Ever hear of a soldier named Bligh?"

"Can't say that I have. What's he look like?"

"About forty-five, tall, fairly well built. A good man with a six gun."

"That's half of the Seventh."

"Bligh's handy with a pack of cards."

"That cuts it down to about a hundred men. What else?"

"That's all I know about him."

21

"You don't know him by sight?"

"I've never laid eyes on him. How about a chap named Morrison, but not the first sergeant of L Troop. A younger man, around thirty-seven, thirty-eight. Probably friendly with Bligh."

"I know Sergeant Morrison, but he's a year or two older'n I am. Came in during the fuss with the Mexicans."

"No, both Bligh and Morrison enlisted within the past four or five years."

"And they're in the Seventh?"

"I'm not sure; they're in the cavalry, that's all I know."

The old soldier snorted. "Then they could be anywhere—Riley, Jefferson Barracks, Leavenworth—maybe even Laramie."

"Yes, they could."

"And they couldda enlisted under other names."

"That's right."

"Then you got a fine chance of findin' 'em!"

Leach nodded thoughtfully. "But I'll find them . . . sometime."

He resumed his work and completed the task shortly after tattoo. In the darkness outside he walked to the M Troop barracks and tiptoed into Squad Room A. He found his bunk, undressed in the darkness, and went to bed.

Five

REVEILLE was at five-thirty and the troop lined up on the parade ground outside the barracks. Leach, not being assigned, took up a position with the noncoms and file closers. The present-or-accounted-fors were called out by the corporals, and reported by the first sergeant to Captain Holterman who made his appearance at the last moment. He went off immediately afterwards and the first sergeant dismissed the troop. Heading back to the barracks, Sergeant O'Hara caught up with Leach.

"What's the idea, Leach?" O'Hara growled. "You shouldda been out in the kitchen a half hour ago."

"Oh, I'm on K.P.?"

"A new man always catches K.P. his first day. Didn't you see your name on the bulletin board?"

"How could I see it?" Leach snapped. "It was dark last night when I got through in the stables."

"It's your business to look at the bulletin board every evening," O'Hara retorted. "Now, hurry up and get out to the kitchen, or you'll really get something worth while."

Seething, Leach went to Squad Room A, took off his uniform and put on fatigue clothes. As he was finishing, Cecil Potts made his appearance, carrying towel, soap and toothbrush. With him was a stocky, swarthy trooper, who turned out to be Fiore, the man who had the bunk on Leach's left. Potts introduced him.

Fiore chuckled. "I see you got K.P."

"O'Hara's riding him," Potts said. "He gave him some stable duty last night before he even got settled."

"That O'Hara," scowled Fiore. "One of these days we'll be out in the field again and maybe O'Hara won't be comin' back."

Potts winced. "None of that talk, Fiore!"

"Every man in the troop's got it in for him," Fiore continued angrily.

23

Leach didn't wait for the rest of the discussion. He hurried out of the squad room and, following his nose, found the kitchen, passing through the mess hall to get to it.

A morose, lean man in cook's outfit sized him up as he entered. "Did the bugler forget to wake you?" he asked sarcastically.

"I didn't know I was on until reveille," Leach explained.

"Oh, no? Well, next time I'll send you an engraved invitation. Now get busy."

There was one other K.P. on duty, a grizzled old soldier, who knew all the shortcuts and performed the duties with a minimum of effort. The tin plates were already set on the tables in the mess hall and the two K.P.'s were kept busy during the next few minutes, carrying buckets of coffee to the tables, huge platters of hot cakes and mountains of bread.

Then the troopers were let in and the K.P.'s were kept scurrying back and forth, fetching refills. There was plenty of food and the sixty-odd soldiers of Troop M did full justice to it.

After breakfast came the washing of the dishes and then a two-hour spell of peeling potatoes. This was followed by the mopping of the mess hall and kitchen and a few miscellaneous chores that the cook managed to find for the K.P.'s. But at last it was ten-thirty and the cook told them morosely:

"Knock off now, but I want you back here at eleven-thirty. Not a minute later; understand?"

Leach went to Squad Room A, found it completely deserted and, after looking over his gear and stowing it away more compactly in his wall locker, left the room. He stood for a moment on the veranda watching a troop of cavalry going through foot maneuvers, then suddenly decided that he needed a couple of items from the sutler's.

He crossed the parade ground and found the sutler's store, a long, low building. He entered and found a half dozen soldiers, off duty, drinking beer at the bar. Quade, the man with the U.S. Grant beard, who had met Molly Quade at the depot in Bismarck, was selling a can of smoking tobacco to a soldier.

Leach stopped to read a notice, announcing a ball, sponsored by Troop B. When he turned away, Molly Quade was behind a counter, watching him.

She smiled at Leach. "That's a very attractive uniform you're wearing."

Leach looked down at his fatigues. "I'll be wearing it most of the time, I imagine. Guess what troop I wound up in?"

"Not . . . ?" Her eyes widened.

"Our friend's, none other. Troop M. Stable duty last night, K.P. today. Tomorrow . . . ?" he shrugged.

The sutler finished with the other trooper, came over. "Dad," exclaimed Molly, "this is the man I was telling you about—the man who fought the soldier yesterday."

The sutler grunted as he sized up Leach. "So you licked O'Hara, eh?" He shook his head. "He's a good man as a rule, a mite too quick with his fists, maybe, but a good soldier. One of the best in the regiment."

"That's Sergeant O'Hara you're talking about?" Leach asked.

"That's right. Oh, Molly's told me about the way he acted toward her, but he'd had a bit too much aboard, I imagine . . ."

"You're defending the man, Dad?" exclaimed Molly.

"And why not? I've known O'Hara for a long time—ever since I came to this post. He pays his bills and he hasn't made me any trouble. Least, not much." He regarded Leach steadily. "Which is more'n I can say for most cavalrymen. They spend five cents for a glass of beer and think it entitles them to break up a dollar's worth of glassware." He grunted. "What is there about soldiers that makes them want to fight all the time? I mean, on their own time, when they're not getting paid for it."

"Father," Molly said somewhat stiffly. "You're forgetting that Mr., I mean, Trooper Leach, had a fight yesterday because—because he came to my rescue."

"I hadn't forgotten it," retorted the sutler. He scowled at Leach. "Thank you, Trooper." And with that he turned and went off to wait upon a cavalryman who had entered.

Molly said to Leach: "Father isn't really as gruff as he pretends to be."

"With a thousand cavalry soldiers, he's got to put up a bluff," Leach conceded. "He had it right about cavalrymen fighting. In the infantry you don't find one half as much fighting among the men."

"How would *you* know, soldier?" Molly asked, with a smile. "You've been in the Army only a matter of twelve or fourteen hours." She cocked her head to one side. "Or, have you been in before?"

"As a matter of fact, yes."

She looked at him thoughtfully. "During the war?"

He nodded.

"I should have known. You're old enough and I wouldn't say you were the type who'd hired a substitute."

"You're too young to know about substitutes," Leach said.

"Oh, am I? Just how old do you think I am?"

"Eighteen—not more."

"I was eighteen, two years ago. Almost three. Besides, my father's been a sutler for eight years."

"But you haven't been with him during all that time?"

"What makes you think I haven't?"

"You didn't know Sergeant O'Hara."

"Oh." She smiled. "You caught me that time. Don't tell anyone, but this is my first day in the Army. I never saw an Army post until last night."

"You haven't lived with your father?"

She shook her head. "I went to live with an aunt, after mother died . . . fourteen years ago. Dad was a freighter on the plains for some years and then he bought a sutlership eight years ago. I've seen him only a half dozen times since mother died. Then Aunt Clara passed away last month, and—well, there wasn't any other place for me to go."

"From what you've seen of Army life, do you think you'll like it?"

"Yes—I'm sure." Her eyes went to the poster on the wall. "I understand there's a dance almost every week. I've been asked four times already this morning to go to the one tonight."

26

"Then you won't have any lack of dancing partners," Leach said.

Her face fell a little at that. Leach was aware of it and looked deliberately at the clock on the wall. "The cook'll be looking for me. Could I get some shaving soap?"

"Of course. I think there's some over here in this counter." She moved aside to the adjoining counter, searched and found the soap. Leach bought two or three other articles, then said: "I have no money. I suppose it's all right . . . ?"

"It's customary, isn't it?"

"It's left up to the sutler. He gets it out of the soldiers' pay. But sometimes he prefers not to give credit to certain soldiers."

"Since I haven't seen *any* money passed this morning, I'm sure *everyone* gets credit here."

"Thanks. Put me down, then. Trooper John Leach, M Troop."

"Very well. And Trooper . . . I didn't say I had accepted any of those four invitations . . ."

He shook his head soberly. "You'd better, because I'm sure Sergeant O'Hara has some plans for me for this evening."

"But he can't—not right after you've been on K.P."

"You'd be surprised what the ranking sergeant of a troop can do."

He smiled thinly. "Have a good time."

He picked up his purchases and left the sutler's store, aware that Molly Quade was staring after him. He crossed the parade ground, re-entered Squad Room A and stowed away his packages. Then he returned to the kitchen and found his fellow K.P. was still missing. But the cook put him to work.

The noon meal was disposed of and about three o'clock the cook again gave the K.P.'s a grudging hour to themselves. Leach used it up in bunk fatigue, then returned to the kitchen and had not a moment's rest until eight o'clock when he and the other K.P. wrung out the last mops and hung them out to dry.

Leach went to the washroom, stripped to his waist and washed himself thoroughly. Then he went up to the squad

27

room and found Troopers Potts and Fiore polishing their boots.

"Dance tonight," Potts said. "Hurry up, we'll wait for you."

"Hasn't Sergeant O'Hara been around looking for me?" Leach asked. "It's only eight o'clock and I'm sure there are some things I could do."

"Not tonight. He left for the dance ten minutes ago."

Leach hesitated a moment, then began peeling off his fatigue clothes. In five minutes he was dressed and ready. "Not bad," said Fiore, the little Italian soldier. "Now, let's hurry before all the girls get taken."

"There's twenty of 'em coming out from Bismarck, I hear," Trooper Potts said cheerfully. "Two ambulance loads."

"You can have 'em," said Fiore. "Me, I was over to the sutler's today." He rolled his eyes. "His daughter's for me."

"The sutler hasn't got a daughter," exclaimed Potts.

Fiore chuckled. "Oh, no? Well, you got a surprise coming to you, but I'm warning you, I saw her first. You try any of your tricks, Limey—"

"Uhuh, even if the sutler has got a daughter, I've seen *him*." He grimaced.

Six

THE dance was being held in a large room two doors from Headquarters. As they passed the latter building, Leach saw lights inside and noted that there were three or four saddled horses tied to the hitchrail outside.

Then they entered the ballroom. They hung their caps on nails just within the door, then stepped forward into the main part of the ballroom, where were congregated some hundred or more troopers and about half that number of women. The regimental band was seated at the far end of the room, playing a waltz.

Fiore caught Leach's arm. "There she is, dancing with—" his face fell—"with Sergeant O'Hara!"

Potts whistled softly. "She's all right, Fiore; for once in your life you didn't exaggerate. But what kind of a girl is she to dance with a skunk like the sergeant?"

"She doesn't know him, that's all," declared Fiore. "But she'll know all about him as soon as I dance with her." Then, as the band stopped playing, "Which'll be the next dance." He started forward across the floor.

Leach, watching, saw O'Hara leading Molly off the floor to the rear of the room. Fiore, cutting in and out, was hurrying to head them off. He saw O'Hara and Molly join a small group that included the sutler. Fiore came up and addressed himself to Molly. Leach saw her smile, shake her head slightly and he imagined that the little trooper stiffened. At any rate, he bowed low, and about-facing, walked off. But he did not come back to Leach and Potts.

"He got turned down," exclaimed Potts.

"I guess I'll try *my* luck," Leach said.

"You?" cried Potts. "With O'Hara hangin' onto her? Why don't you just put a gun to your head? It'll be quicker—and easier."

But Leach was already crossing the floor. As he approached he saw that the group about Molly consisted entirely of noncommissioned officers and all of them vying for the attention of the sutler's daughter.

Then she looked past O'Hara and saw Leach bearing down. A pleased expression flitted across her face, but she erased it quickly.

Leach came up and bowing, asked: "Could I have the pleasure of the next dance?"

"Why, yes," she replied. "Sergeant O'Hara was to dance with me, but since I just had the last with him, I'm sure he won't mind—"

That was as far as she got. O'Hara, whirling, saw Leach. "You," he snarled, "what are *you* doing here?"

"Why, I've just asked Miss Quade to dance with me," Leach replied.

"I heard . . . and I *do* mind. Molly, I'm holding you to your promise."

"I don't recall making any promise," Molly retorted. "In fact, I don't even think I agreed to dance the next one with you."

O'Hara's face turned dark in sudden rage. But before he could speak again, the band started playing and Molly stepped out toward Leach.

Leach took her hand and led her out upon the floor. "So you made friends with him," he said, quietly accusing.

"What could I do? He came to the canteen this afternoon, apologized and . . ." A slight frown creased her smooth features. "You heard Father this morning about O'Hara. Thinks he's the salt of the earth—in spite of what O'Hara did yesterday."

"I see," said Leach thoughtfully.

"But let's not talk about Sergeant O'Hara," exclaimed Molly. "This is my first Army dance and I want to remember it." For a moment or two she danced quietly, smoothly, with Leach, then he caught her looking at him.

He grinned. "I'm glad I was able to make it."

"So am I. I've been thinking about you, John Leach. I guess I talked to a hundred soldiers today, at the store. Privates, corporals, sergeants—officers . . ."

"And . . . ?"

30

"And I've been thinking, there's something dis- tinguishes the officers from the enlisted men. Even the sergeants. They lack something the officers have, a sureness about them. They carry themselves differently, the officers, I mean."

"The enlisted man's stiff," Leach said. "He gets that from drill, standing at attention, saluting officers. The caste system, in the Army, is strong. Like this dance; it's for enlisted men, not officers. And the officers' dances won't permit enlisted men—"

"I know all that, John," exclaimed Molly. "But *you've* got it, the ease and carelessness of the officer. You said you'd been in the army before—you were an officer, weren't you . . . ?"

Leach took two or three steps before he replied. Then he said: "Yes."

"I knew it! But why—why did you enlist as a private this time? Why didn't you try for a commission?"

"It isn't so easy to get a commission in the peacetime army," Leach said. "Even when there are vacancies. You've got to pass certain examinations."

"Could you pass them?"

"Perhaps. I don't know. But I don't know that I want to be an officer. If I wanted to make a career of the army—"

"You mean you just enlisted . . . for a little while?"

A faint smile crossed Leach's lips. "Five years. Not such a little while."

"Then why don't you try for the commission?"

Leach never got to answer that question. In the middle of the waltz the band suddenly went into a fanfare. In the abrupt silence that followed, a loud voice said:

"Attention, men of Troop M. You are wanted at your barracks immediately. Men of Troop M, report to your barracks at once."

"That's me," Leach said to Molly.

"What does it mean?"

"Hardly a drill."

"The troop can't be going out, at this time of the night?"

31

"I wouldn't be too sure of that. Well . . . goodbye, if I don't see you again for awhile."

He gave her a half salute and walked off. Outside, soldiers were already hurrying across the parade ground. The barracks of M Troop were ablaze with lights and when Leach entered Squad Room A men on all sides had packs spread out on their cots and on the floor and were rolling them up.

Corporal Stockbridge looked up from strapping a neatly rolled pack. "You got twenty minutes, Leach," he snapped.

"For what?"

"To get ready for marching."

"What's up?"

Stockbridge winked. "The general told me, but said I should keep it a secret."

Leach hurried across the room and there found Potts and Fiore already getting their gear in order.

"We ride!" exulted the Englishman.

"Any chance of action?"

"There's always a chance, out here in the Dakotas. When Custer said there was gold in the Black Hills he practically declared war. The Indians say the white man can't enter the Black Hills, but try to keep out a white man if he thinks there's gold anywhere."

The little Italian, Fiore, snapped at Leach: "You did all right with the sutler's daughter, I noticed."

Leach grinned. "I forgot to tell you—I met her on the train yesterday. In fact, she was the cause of my fight with O'Hara."

Potts stared at Leach. "You had a real fight with O'Hara? But you're not even marked up and he—"

"I won."

Fiore vaulted clear across his bunk and stared up at Leach. "*You* licked O'Hara?"

The Englishman whistled softly. "No wonder he's got it in for you!"

"And Stockbridge," Leach added in a low tone.

"You beat the two of them?"

"Stockbridge didn't really count. I merely slapped him down."

32

Potts came up close to Leach. "Then watch yourself, if we get into action."

"I'll watch him," spat out Fiore. "And I'll watch O'Hara, too. I've got it in for him and if he tries any funny stuff . . ."

A bugle split the night and whistles in the barracks began to blast. Noncoms, in the various squad rooms, yelled: "Fall out, M Troop!"

The troop formed quickly on the parade ground. It was the only troop outside, so apparently the maneuver would involve M Troop alone. The non-commissioned officers made their reports, there was a quick search for delinquents and then, well within a half hour from the time of the first announcement in the dance hall, the troop marched to the stables. Horses were saddled and the troop formed again upon the parade ground.

Leach drew a powerful gelding, which had a bit more fight than he cared for, inasmuch as he had not been in a saddle for a couple of years. But he thought he could manage the animal. Ammunition, both carbine and revolver, was issued and then the bugler blew "Boots and Saddles."

M Troop mounted.

Captain Holterman sized up his troop and gave an order to the first sergeant, who repeated it. Then it ran through the platoon sergeants and corporals.

The troop marched, riding through the gates of Fort Lincoln, out onto the Dakota prairie land.

Leach, still a file-closer, found himself riding behind Sergeant O'Hara, but they had gone a mile or more before O'Hara seemed to notice him. Then he allowed his horse to fall back beside Leach's.

"Little party I'm putting on for you, special," he said thinly. "Hope you like it."

"Sioux?"

"Yep. And you know what? They don't fight with their fists. Oh—I forgot, you're an old soldier. Fought all through the Big War. Captain, too, weren't you?"

"That's a long time ago, O'Hara."

"Sure. Maybe you forgot what a bullet sounds like. Although I hear these little playmates didn't just use guns

33

today. Arrows, lances. Ever see a lance wound? Or what the Indians do to their prisoners?"

"What," asked Leach, "would it take to make you lay off, O'Hara?"

The sergeant chuckled wickedly. "The pleasure of reporting you A.W.O.L."

"That you won't get."

"I think maybe I will. I've been studying you, Leach. You're a gentleman, underneath. You can only take so much."

"I can take as much as you can dish out, O'Hara."

"The Seventh Cavalry isn't big enough for the two of us."

Leach lapsed into silence. There was no use bandying words with O'Hara. The sergeant was a man who knew how to hate. Nothing would assuage that hate. Nothing but the utter destruction of the cause of it. John Leach.

O'Hara rode back to his position and the troop continued on into the night.

Shortly after dawn a halt was called and the troopers dismounted and stretched cramped muscles.

Seven

THE edge of the sun was creeping up over the eastern horizon, but in all directions Leach saw nothing but undulating prairie. No, there was a thread of smoke to the north and west. He watched it for a moment, then caught the eye of Trooper Cecil Potts.

"Smoke," he said, nodding.

"Damned if it isn't." The Englishman's eyes went to the head of the column, where Captain Holterman was gathered in a small group with the two lieutenants, the top sergeant and an Arikari guide.

Near by, O'Hara was conversing in low tones with Corporal Stockbridge. Potts looked at them and said to Leach, "Somebody ought to tell the skipper about the smoke."

"They'll see it."

"It may be important. Know why we're out?"

"Sioux, I suppose."

"Naturally; but they're out in pretty strong force. Bunch of about fifty attacked a wagon train yesterday. Twelve people in it, four women. Killed them all." Potts frowned then suddenly started for the head of the column.

As he came up to Stockbridge and O'Hara, the latter suddenly shot out an arm and blocked the Englishman. "Hold your place, Potts."

"Sure," said Potts, "and I was only going to report to the captain that there's a bit of smoke goin' up there to the north and west . . ."

O'Hara wheeled, searched the horizon and finding the thread of smoke, exclaimed, "What of it? I've seen it for the last five minutes." But he turned on his heel and started for the head of the column.

Leach, watching, saw him salute the officers, then talk and point toward the smoke. He could not hear the conversation, but knew that they were discussing the discovery. A moment later the command rang out:

"Prepare to mount!"

The troop was off again, but the route had been changed from due west to north and west. And the Arikari and a corporal went ahead of the column. They separated after awhile, the Arikari heading directly for the smoke and the trooper going in a more westerly direction.

The pace of the troop was swifter, now, and the skirmishers rode out further to the right and left. The smoke became plainer for awhile, then faded and after ten or fifteen minutes could be seen no more.

An hour after sunrise the Arikari returned to the troop, driving his horse at a swift lope. He talked to the captain for a moment, and then the command came to put the tired cavalry horses into a trot, a command that at this time indicated extreme urgency.

The troop crested a rise in the ground and the soldiers saw ahead and below the cause of the smoke, although the smoke itself now consisted only of a few wisps here and there.

A half mile ahead lay what was left of a wagon train. Black, charred wood, twisted iron and steel, shreds of scorched canvas and a number of huddled bodies.

The troop covered the remaining distance at a gallop. Arriving at the scene of the massacre, scouts and vedettes were thrown out before the order to dismount was given.

The embers were still warm to the touch, the wagon tires hot. The bodies still had the blood, uncongealed. There were nineteen, including three women and two children. All had been scalped, most of them mutilated.

"The bloody heathens," Trooper Potts swore softly.

Fiore's swarthy face was two shades lighter. "I still say Sheridan's got the right idea; kill every goddam Indian in the West and you'll get peace. They're savages and that's the way we ought to treat them." His eyes were on the mutilated body of one of the children.

The bugler blew a couple of notes on his trumpet, somewhat to the surprise of the troopers. But looking toward the captain, they saw him signal for the men to assemble.

36

"We should bury them," he announced, "but we're not going to take the time. This happened at dawn and it's my guess that the scoundrels are less than an hour ahead of us. Our horses are pretty worn, but it's my hunch they've gone into camp not so far from here, and if they have, we'll get them. Dance-in-Rain, how many would you say there were?"

The Arikari looked at the ground, spat and shrugged. "Maybe twenty."

Captain Holterman exclaimed. "Twenty Indians wouldn't have killed all of these people, unless they caught them completely by surprise and the signs don't indicate that they did."

Dance-in-Rain spat again. "Maybe hundred. Maybe hundred and fifty."

The captain scowled and turned his back on the Indian. "Prepare to mount!" he ordered.

The troop mounted and quickly got back into columns of twos. Captain Holterman threw out additional skirmishers, with instructions to come in the moment they sighted a single Indian, and then the troop was off.

The horses, having rested a few minutes, were in better shape and the troop made swift progress toward the west. The trail of the Indians was easy to follow. Knickknacks, clothing, edibles taken from the burned wagon train, scattered the trail.

The country became more hilly and Captain Holterman pulled down the pace of the troop after awhile. There was no sense in rushing headlong into an ambush. There were a half dozen skirmishers ahead and if they sighted Indians they would let the troop know soon enough.

Finally, after more than an hour of traveling from the scene of the massacre, a skirmisher was sighted galloping back. Captain Holterman promptly stopped the troop.

Beyind the first skirmisher came another.

The soldiers talked to the captain for a moment, then wheeling their horses, rode back the way they had come. The captain signaled for the troop to advance again, at a walk.

The head of the troop crested a low hill and came to a halt. In low tones the sergeants, then the corporals, gave

37

the order to advance on a front. In a few minutes the entire troop was spread along the top of the hill.

A quarter mile ahead was a broad shallow stream in the center of which was a small, wooded island. Halfway down the hill, toward the stream, the skirmishers had halted, a half dozen men widely scattered.

When they saw the troop deployed upon the hill, the skirmishers, as if by a signal, turned their horses and, converging, rode back.

As the first man approached, he called out: "Indians on the island, Captain!"

"How many?"

"Don't know, but they've seen us and they haven't lit out."

A second skirmisher came up. "They're prepared to fight, sir."

The captain studied the wooded island with his glasses. On each side of him, the lieutenants were doing the same.

The captain lowered his glasses. "I don't count more than twenty horses."

The Arikari scout grunted. "Maybe twenty. Maybe hundred."

The captain addressed the first lieutenant: "From the trail I'd guess closer to the hundred, wouldn't you?"

"Easily that, sir. Did you examine the ridge on the far side of the island?"

"Yes, and I don't like it. Nor do I like the thought of twenty Indians trying to fight this troop."

"It could be a trap. Wait ... they're mounting their horses ... !"

Captain Holterman nodded grimly. "I wish they'd charge us. This is a good position. We'll dismount and—" He broke off and whipped the glasses to his face. "They're retreating!"

That was apparent now, even to the troopers not possessed of glasses. Mounted Indians suddenly charged from the island to the open beyond, their horses splashing through not more than a foot of water. Although the range was prohibitive the Indians began banging away with their guns, as they fled.

38

"Troop attention!" cried Captain Holterman. "At a trot, forward—ho!"

M Troop went down the hillside toward the stream, a quarter of a mile away. They rode on a compact front, at a brisk trot, ready for a charge, or for retreat.

On the far side of the river, the Indians suddenly halted, halfway toward the crest of the ridge. They milled about for a moment, then spread out into a semblance of a front and fired a ragged volley in the general direction of the advancing troopers.

An eighth of a mile from the river, Captain Holterman gave an order to the bugler and he brought the troop to a halt with a quick call.

"I don't like it," Holterman said to his lieutenants. "Twenty Indians who've started to run away wouldn't stop like that in the face of a troop of cavalry."

"You're right, sir," said the first lieutenant. "I don't think we should cross that river until we know what's behind that ridge."

And then, suddenly, they knew. One moment the ridge was bare, the next it was thickly studded with mounted warriors, appearing as if from under the horizon.

They came charging down the steep slope at a full gallop, hundreds of them.

"A trap!" roared Captain Holterman. He swiveled in his saddle, shot a quick glance back at the slope that the troop had recently vacated. It was about the same distance, now, as the river, and offered a good defensive position.

But the island in the river offered a better one.

"Forward!" cried Captain Holterman. "To the island—at a gallop!"

Forward the troop went, at a thundering gallop. The smaller group of Indians, who had led the troop on, were closer to the river and the island than the soldiers, and they saw the intent of the troop and charged forward, well ahead of the main body of Indians. Behind them came five hundred Sioux, yelling, whooping and shooting.

The troop hit the shallow water and went across it without faltering. They reached the sandy island, a hundred feet across the water and began leaping headlong from their horses. The small group of Indians were a few yards ahead of them, but when the soldiers went for them, with carbines and spitting six shooters, they broke and fled. Not more than half of them reached the water and only three or four of those got safely across.

"Down," came the command. "Use whatever shelter you can find and fire at will."

The Indian horde hit the water and enveloped itself in the spray of water created by two thousand splashing hooves. But the soldiers knew where to fire and spray did not turn bullets.

Forward the Indians came, whooping and firing. The soldiers were down on the sand. They were armed with Spencer repeating carbines, each weapon capable of firing seven times without reloading. And then they had six shooters for closer range.

A storm of lead met the Indians as they hit the water, increased as they advanced across the hundred feet of the shallow stream and became a veritable hurricane as they approached the little island and came within revolver range.

The splashes in the water now were caused by Indian bodies. Horses went down, dying and wounded, threshed about and screamed in awful anguish. The weight of the Indians behind pressed on those in front, but the front line was melting under the hail of death.

Suddenly, when several Indians had actually touched the sandy soil of the island, the charge broke. For an instant the Indians milled madly, then the general movement was to the rear.

"Let them have it!" The cry went up among the troopers and the soldiers rose to their feet and blazed away with everything they had.

The Indians reached the shore, but they left a good many of their number in the shallow waters and they lost a half dozen men more as they fled up the slope to the ridge, just out of accurate carbine range.

"Cease firing!" yelled Captain Holterman to his troopers. "We've beaten them off, but they'll charge again as soon as they reform. It'll be a stronger charge than the last. Get out your entrenching tools and dig—dig!"

Eight

THE soldiers realized well the gravity of their position and they threw down their carbines and began digging in the soft sand. They used trench tools, a few shovels, knives and even their hands. They worked furiously. All except two troopers who would work no more and a half dozen who were having wounds bandaged.

Up on the ridge the Indians were forming a line of battle. They created a front at least a hundred feet wide and five horses deep. The formation consumed less than five minutes of time and then the second charge began.

Warned by the bugle, the men of M Troop threw down their spades and other trench tools, dove for the shallow pits they had dug and caught up their rifles.

"Hold your fire until I give the command!" Captain Holterman ordered. He had himself appropriated a carbine from one of the dead men and was in one of the front pits, lying beside a trooper.

Down the hill came the whooping and yelling Indians. Bullets whistled through the trees of the island, smacked into wood, or plunked into sand. Horses were hit, screamed and plunged about, but the soldiers remained in their pits, grim and watchful.

The first rank of Indians hit the water, a hundred feet away.

"Steady!" cautioned Holterman. "We've got to stop them this time."

The fire of the Indians became more deafening. Here and there a prone soldier was hit by a wild bullet. One trooper, unable to restrain himself, fired and dropped an Indian from his horse. But the rest of the troop obeyed the captain's order.

Closer the Indians came. Seventy feet, sixty. . . .

Fifty.

"Fire!" roared Captain Holterman.

41

A solid sheet of fire and death belched from the little island, caught the front rank of the charging Indians and almost completely decimated it. Horses and men went down by tens, scores. The entire line of charging Indians became a maelstrom of falling horses and men, overridden by and intermingling with the second line of battle.

Frantically, the soldiers on the island pumped out empty cartridges, injected fresh ones into breeches. The second volley was a bit more irregular than the first but only slightly less lethal. A score of Indian ponies went down, with almost twice that number of Indians. Riderless horses plunged and reared, galloped aimlessly forward, sidewards.

And again the soldiers poured in their deadly fire.

Single Indians reached the island, went down under point-blank fire. One or two threw themselves from their horses and dove for soldiers, but were quickly disposed of.

A hundred Indians went down in that inferno of fire and death poured forth from the island. Some were only wounded, and fled on foot, or caught hold of riderless horses. Some remained in the water, reddening the shallow stream.

The charge melted away. No red men could stand such a withering blast of death. Rifles they understood; they had guns themselves. Some were even possessed of repeating rifles, but a solid troop of entrenched men with repeating rifles that fired over and over in seconds was too much for any Indian charge.

The Indians fled back to the mainland, up to the crest where they were out of range.

On the island the troopers sat up to count their own losses. Horses were down everywhere, others wounded, were dashing about aimlessly, crashing here and there to earth.

Wounded men there were. And dead men. Too many of each. Eight dead now, almost half of the survivors with at least one wound. Captain Holterman sat up and examined a bloody thigh. The first lieutenant was dead. First Sergeant Parker was dying from three wounds.

Little Fiore, in the shallow pit beside John Leach had a

42

flesh wound in his left forearm. He was tying it up with a dirty handkerchief, swearing softly to himself.

Leach was one of the fortunate ones. He had come out of the two Indian charges completely unscathed.

"Here," he said to Fiore, "let me do that for you."

He took up the little man's arm, twisted the handkerchief tightly about the arm and knotted it securely. "As good as new."

"I got at least three of 'em, so help me!" Fiore exclaimed. "I got that big buck with all the feathers. Musta been Sittin' Bull himself."

Trooper Potts crawled over from a neighboring pit. A trickle of blood seeped down his face from a scratch on his forehead, but otherwise he was unwounded.

"Join the cavalry!" he chanted. "Join the United States Cavalry and see the life on the Great Plains." He sat down in the hole and wiped his perspiring forehead. "I thought the Fuzzy-Wuzzies in Africa were fighting fools, but these redskins are ten times worse. The way they charged into our bloomin' guns. . . . Ten seconds more and we wouldn't be talkin' about it right now."

"Do you think they'll come again?" Leach asked.

The Englishman shook his head. "I hardly think so. Time means nothing to them and they know they've got us tied down. We haven't got horses for twenty men and with our wounded . . . No, we're sewed down here."

He ducked to one side as a bullet plunked into the sand only a couple of feet from his legs. "Oh-oh, now comes the sniping!"

The Indians, reassembled on top of the ridge, two hundred yards or so from the island, now began banging away at the besieged troopers. The range was just a little too far for accurate fire—accurate for Indians, notoriously bad marksmen, but the island was small and the number of the snipers was large and bullets that were aimed at one man could just as well hit another.

The soldiers got down into their rifle pits and lying prone or on their sides, dug them deeper, throwing the sand into parapets in front of them. The horses, unfortunately, were unprotected and they suffered the most damage.

The Indians did not charge again, but ten minutes of desultory firing accounted for every horse on the island. Another man or two was hit, but in general the soldiers had burrowed themselves down into comparative safety.

About an hour after the second charge, the Indians made a decisive move, although it was not necessarily a vital one to the beleaguered troopers. Almost half of the Indians moved downstream, three or four hundred yards and there crossed. They moved back upstream and took up a position on the hill where Captain Holterman had originally planned to make a stand. It was almost a quarter of a mile from the island, but bodies of the Indians moved down closer to the river and galloped their horses back and forth, making feints toward the island, but always remaining just out of rifle shot.

The soldiers fired at the Indians occasionally to discourage them, but on the whole conserved their ammunition. The Indians kept up a continual, spasmodic firing.

It was hot on the island, lying in the sand. The wounded got the water from the canteens and the unwounded began suffering from lack of water.

The situation of M Troop was precarious. Captain Holterman summed it up in midafternoon with Lieutenant Gregson, the sole officer on the island who remained unharmed.

"K Troop is supposed to move out tomorrow," he said, "but the plan was for them to patrol south and west. They won't come within thirty miles of us here."

"What do you make it to the fort, Captain?" the lieutenant asked.

"Fifty miles, a few more or less. We moved pretty steadily during the night and we must have covered ten miles today. In fact, I think sixty miles would be more like it."

"A good man could make it on foot in twenty hours."

"I know; I've been thinking. The Indians will move down to the water as soon as it gets dark, but still there's a hundred feet on the west and almost that much on the east side. A man would have a chance of getting down to the water, then circle around and get behind the Indians and head out for the fort. He could get there by dark and

44

the relief column could make it here by morning. Forty hours. We've enough rations and after dark we can fill the canteens. . . . How's the ammunition?"

"Not too good, sir. We could stand one more charge, but not much more. However, I think the Indians have had enough of that. They lost a hundred men or more in those two charges."

"I know. They don't know our own losses and I don't think they'll have the stomach for another try."

But they did. The Indians, believing a charge from both sides of the water could succeed, made one more try in the late afternoon. It wasn't as determined a charge as the second one of that morning, but the garrison on the island was greatly depleted and the charge came close to succeeding—closer than the Indians realized. In fact, if it hadn't been for the wounded, even some who were seriously wounded, firing rifles as fast as they could manage, the Indians would have overrun the island.

They didn't succeed and lost thirty or forty men in the attempt, but the death toll on the island was increased by six more men and many more wounded. Less than fifteen men remained untouched and the captain, himself, received another wound, which incapacitated him completely. Lieutenant Gregson took over command.

Crouched in a rifle pit he talked to the surviving noncommissioned officers. "I don't have to tell any of you the spot we're in. It couldn't be worse. We're all right until morning, but if the Indians make one more charge we're done. I don't think they will and we've got to play it from that supposition. I want some volunteers to try to get through. . . ."

Every one of the four surviving noncommissioned officers promptly volunteered.

"I'll risk two of you," Lieutenant Gregson said, "but I need a couple of enlisted men, too. K Troop will be riding out tomorrow. We've got to try to intercept them, but on foot it's going to be easy to miss them. However, we'll try, but we'll need a couple of men to head directly for the fort. At intervals, in case the first don't get through. O'Hara, you know the country pretty well, you'll try to contact K Troop. Plennert, you'll take off an hour after

O'Hara. Now, I want two men to go for the fort. It's not necessary that they know the country as well. They'll just have to head straight east and south, a little. It's a good stiff hike, but I don't see how they can miss the fort once they hit the trails. They all lead to the fort. Sergeant O'Hara will you call for a couple of volunteers?"

"Yes, sir."

O'Hara crawled out of the rifle pit and on hands and knees scuttled for a trench, in which Fiore, Leach, Potts and another trooper lay.

"Ah, me brave Indian fighters," the sergeant chuckled. "And how do you like this business? Anything like Yellow Tavern? Or Richmond?"

"Some good men died today," Trooper Potts said, disgustedly, "but I don't see even a scratch on the likes of you."

"You look pretty good yourself, Limey," retorted O'Hara. "Fit for a nice bit of rescue work. The lieutenant says volunteers only, but I'm sure you'll volunteer."

"Of course."

"What about me?" growled little Fiore.

"You've got a bum leg, Fiore." O'Hara looked at Leach.

Leach nodded. The fourth trooper snapped. "What about me?"

"Too late, son. Potts and Leach are fine able-bodied men. We need two. Come along, brave lads."

O'Hara crawled out of the pit, followed by Leach and Potts. The lieutenant's pit was a tight fit, but the three men squirmed in.

The lieutenant shook his head when he saw Leach. "You're the recruit. I got a glimpse of you during the last charge and you did very well, but I think this job requires a more experienced soldier—."

"Four years with the 32nd Missouri, sir," Leach said, promptly.

"Under the General hisself," O'Hara backed up Leach. "He outranked yourself, no less. A captain."

"Well," said the lieutenant, looking at Leach with interest. "I didn't know. In fact, we'll have to talk about that. Later. All right, you'll do. You and Sergeant O'Hara will go downstream first. O'Hara goes to try to intercept K Troop somewhere to the south. You'll head for the fort. An hour after you've gone, Sergeant Plennert and Trooper Potts follow. You'll take your revolvers, but I don't think carbines will be practical."

Night fell swiftly over the island in the middle of the river. The troopers saw campfires go up on the two ridges that hemmed them in and knew that the Indians would be eating cooked meat. Some of them would be sleeping and resting, but for those on the island there would be little of either. Rations, they had, and water, now that they were able to fill their canteens under cover of the darkness.

In a pit at the water's edge, Sergeant O'Hara and Leach prepared themselves. They divested themselves of blouses and caps and revolver belts. O'Hara tied a handkerchief rather tightly about his throat and thrust his Colt's revolver into the back of it, so the six rounds of ammunition that it contained would not get wet. Leach went through the same operation and then Lieutenant Gregson shook hands with both of them.

"I don't have to tell you what this means. Taking unnecessary chances may mean the death of every man here. Speed isn't as important as getting through. Good luck."

Nine

THE two men crawled into the shallow water and remained still for a moment. An Indian on the west shore let go with a rifle, but as the shot was not taken up by others, the men in the water assumed that it was merely fired for morale purposes and after a moment moved off in the water.

The water wasn't deep enough to swim or even float and the men had to crawl along on hands and knees, slowly, carefully, in order not to make a splash. In places the water was no more than an inch or two deep, but fortunately the bottom of the creek was sandy and the going was not as difficult as if it had been mud. Against this, however, were the Indian campfires up on the ridges and close to the water farther downstream. They created enough light so that moving objects could be seen in the river, if anyone was watching.

Detection was certain death, a fact of which the two men in the water did not need to remind themselves. In the first half hour they proceeded less than a hundred yards.

O'Hara, who was in the lead, then waited for Leach to catch up to him. "The water seems to be deeper along the west bank," he whispered. "And there's a bit of an overhanging bank. I think we'd move faster under it."

Leach made no reply but as the sergeant worked his way to the right side of the stream, he followed. O'Hara was right, the water was two feet deep and in spots even deeper and there was a bank of the same general height overhanging the water.

The two men were able to get to their feet and by crouching low doubled their speed. In another half hour they were a quarter mile downstream. The water became shallower again, but emboldened by their success so far

48

the two soldiers remained on their feet and proceeded another quarter of a mile.

Then Sergeant O'Hara climbed out of the water. "We part here," he said. "It's just as well for me to stay on this side of the river, but your best bet is to cross now and head for the east." He pointed to the edge of an almost full moon that was coming up over the eastern horizon. "There's your direction."

Leach nodded, turned away, but O'Hara called softly to him. "Don't get the idea that this ends our little fight. I'm merely postponing it."

Leach made no reply, but stooping, crossed the river. At the low bank he paused for a moment and strained his ears. Had he heard a sound?

If so, it was not repeated.

The outskirts of the Indian camps were almost a mile upriver. There were no doubt single Indians roaming about, but Leach was on the alert, ready to sink to the ground in an instant. He was dripping wet and the night was chilly, but movement would keep him warm.

He took the revolver from his neckcloth, started to thrust it into the waistband of his trousers, then believing the moisture might creep into the cartridges, decided to carry it in his hand.

He struck out eastward, walking with long strides, but bent over to form as small a silhouette against the skyline as possible. He walked a hundred yards from the river and stopping, suddenly turned in his tracks.

A hundred feet away, a blob of shadow dropped to the ground. Leach threw himself to the ground, cocking his revolver at the same time. Flame lanced toward him from the darkness and a revolver split the stillness of the night.

Leach groaned inwardly. The shot would bring other Indians. The safest place was the river, but it was a hundred yards away and he had to pass or skirt his attacker. Yet to remain where he was was too dangerous.

A voice suddenly called: "Soldier!"

A white man's voice.

Leach tensed himself. "Yes?"

Fire split the darkness once more and sand splattered

49

Leach's face. But then he was on his knees, triggering his own gun. Once, twice.

A figure leaped up, a hundred yards away. Leach snapped a third shot at it, a fourth, then held his fire. The range was too far for accurate revolver shooting at night—and the man who had stalked him was fleeing rapidly toward the river.

Leach's impulse was to go after the attempted assassin, but thought of his mission deterred him. Instead, he whirled and bent low started running eastward as swiftly as he could. He ran a quarter mile, then dropped and pressed his ear to the ground.

He caught the faint drumming of horses' hoofs, but although he listened for a moment or two, the hoofbeats did not become appreciably louder and Leach knew that they were following the river bank, which he had vacated only a short time ago.

He got to his feet and began running again. An eighth of a mile and he went down and listened again. He could still hear the hoofs pounding the prairie, but they were even fainter than before. He got up again and this time ran a full half mile. When he listened he could no longer hear the drumming of the hoofs.

He got up and drawing a great breath began walking. He had to conserve his strength, for sixty miles lay ahead of him.

He walked steadily for three hours and judged that he had covered eleven or twelve miles from the river. The moon was high in the sky and the prairie was almost as light as day. He stopped for five minutes and threw himself down upon the grass to rest.

Rising, he again started his eastward journey and walked until the sky in the east turned grey. Then he enjoyed ten or fifteen minutes rest. When he got up, dawn was breaking in the east.

It was a half hour later that he saw the two horsemen on the horizon. There was a shallow buffalo wallow a few yards away. Bent low, Leach raced for it.

In the depression he watched the horsemen. They were approaching him and before many minutes Leach made

50

out that they were Indians. The way they were coming they would pass him within a hundred yards.

Leach burrowed down into the wallow and strained his ears to listen. The Indian ponies were traveling at an easy lope, but suddenly the beat of their hoofs stopped. Leach knew that he had to risk a look. Cautiously he raised his eyes above the low parapet of the wallow.

Fifty yards away, the two Indians sat on their ponies, looking directly at Leach's hiding spot. Even as Leach saw them, the Indians let out a yell and charged.

Leach scrambled to his knees, thrust forward his revolver and in that instant remembered that he had but two cartridges in his gun. He could not afford to miss.

One of the Indians had a long rifle, which he was trying to aim at Leach; the other seemed to be armed only with a lance. Leach covered the one with the rifle, stepped swiftly aside at the moment he guessed the man was about to shoot and avoided the bullet that came.

Then Leach fired. For an instant he held his breath, then groaned aloud as he realized he had missed. He cocked the revolver the second time, waited until the charging Indians were no more than thirty feet away, then fired the second and last time.

The Indian with the rifle plummeted to the ground, but his horse came on. Leach, ducking frantically aside, escaped from being knocked down by the horse. The second Indian, armed only with the lance, overran Leach, but whirling his pony on hind legs, came back at him.

The gun in Leach's hand was empty, there wasn't time to get the dead Indian's single shot rifle and load it. Leach backed away and the Indian, seeming to sense that Leach was at a disadvantage let out a whoop and charged, the lance pointed for Leach's body.

Leach drew back the heavy six shooter and threw it at the Indian's head. He missed, but the throw saved his life, for it caused the Indian to jerk his head aside and the point of the lance barely grazed the side of Leach's body.

Leach turned with the lance, grabbed at it with both hands and gaining a savage hold, dug his heels into the ground. The Indian pony bumped against him, but Leach,

51

holding for his life, jerked the Indian from the pony's back.

The man landed heavily, bounced up, turned a complete somersault, and came to his feet, with his tomahawk raised.

For an instant the two men, red and white, faced each other at a distance of a dozen feet. Leach had a lance, the other man a tomahawk.

The Indian's hand went back for a throw and then Leach lunged forward with the lance. A numbing blow struck his left shoulder, but it was too late. The momentum of Leach's rush carried him forward. The point of the lance entered the Indian's breast, went clear through his body.

Leach let go of the lance, staggered aside and watched the death struggle of the Indian. Then he sat down, shaking. After a few minutes, he peeled back his shirt and looked at his shoulder. The blunt edge of the ax had hit him and the skin was not even broken, but the flesh was an angry red. In a while it would turn black. He tested his shoulder and winced at the pain, but got heavily to his feet.

The first Indian lay off a short distance. Leach walked over, found that the rifle was an ancient muzzle loader and decided that he was just as well off without it. It would only hamper his speed in traveling.

The horses.

Leach made a complete circle, saw them both scampering off in the distance. Without a rope it was useless even to attempt to catch one.

It was late afternoon when Leach caught sight of a sod house a mile or so to the north. He shifted his course and, as he approached the house, saw a horse in a pole corral. He broke into a run, heading for the corral instead of the house. As he reached it, a man came running out, but Leach, ignoring him, climbed the poles and dropped down into the corral.

"Here you," cried the settler, "what do you think you're doing?"

Leach, already heading for the horse, spoke over his shoulder. "I need your horse—I've got to get to the fort

52

as quickly as possible. My troop's surrounded by Indians . . ."

"Indians! Where . . . ?"

"To the west; I've been walking all night. . . ."

"Take the horse! Leave him at the fort and I'll pick him up later." The man climbed through the poles. "Here—let me catch him for you . . ."

He caught up a bridle from a post and approached the animal, which had shied away from Leach but let his master come up. The man slipped the bit into the animal's mouth, began strapping on the bridle.

"I've got a saddle in the house. . . ."

"Can't take the time," Leach said. He caught hold of the bridle and vaulted up on the bare back of the horse. "Open the gate."

The man ran for the corral gate, let down the bars. "Are they—I mean, is there any chance of their coming this close . . . ?"

"No," said Leach. "The entire Seventh will be out after them in a day or two. They'll wipe 'em from the plains."

He touched the horse's flank with the heel of a boot and the animal sprang through the gate.

Ten

AN hour later, Leach rode past the sentry at the gates of Fort Lincoln and brought his tired mount to an abrupt halt in front of Headquarters.

Major Comstock, coming out just at that moment, saw Leach, blinked and exclaimed. "Say—aren't you in M Troop . . . ?"

Leach sprang to the ground and saluted. "Yes sir, I've just come from the troop; we're cut off sixty miles from here. Half of our men are already down—"

"How many Indians?" roared the major.

"Five hundred, sir. Perhaps more. . . ."

"Wait . . .!"

The major whirled, dashed into Headquarters. He had scarcely disappeared than the corporal clerk came dashing out. He shot past Leach, heading for the guardhouse at a dead run.

The major popped out of Headquarters again. "What's the position, Leach? Is there—any chance?"

"Yes sir, if the Indians didn't make another charge today. We beat them off three times yesterday, with extremely heavy losses. The last charge wasn't too strong. The troop's on an island in the middle of a river. . . ."

"I know the place. Rode past there only a month ago. If Captain Holterman—"

"He's down, sir. Badly wounded. Lieutenant Gregson's in command. . . ."

A bugler came dashing out of the guardhouse. He put his trumpet to his lips and blew "Boots and Saddles." Instantly the fort was the scene of tremendous activity. Men by the hundreds came dashing out of buildings, rushed into others. Horses appeared from the direction of the stables. Officers dashed past enlisted men and the latter did not salute.

A captain came rushing up to Major Comstock. "What is it, Major?"

"M Troop—in a bad way. This man's just come. We've got to move out. Where's the colonel?"

The captain, looking past the major, pointed. "Coming!"

Leach turned and saw him striding toward the group in front of Headquarters; Lieutenant Colonel George Armstrong Custer, the nominal head of the famous Seventh Cavalry. Custer, the one-time Boy General. Hero of Gettysburg, Yellow Tavern, the Shenandoah, the man who broke the last lines at Appomattox Courthouse and demanded the surrender of the Army of Virginia from Old Longstreet himself.

Longhair, Scourge of the Plains. Indian fighter. Hero of the Washita, friend of Sheridan, Sherman and Grant, once court-martialed and soon to face a court for a second time and within a year—Little Big Horn.

He strode up, tall and rawboned, his long yellow hair and fierce mustaches in fine contrast to his exotic self-designed uniform.

"What's going on?" he demanded when still several paces away.

" 'Boots and Saddles,' sir," responded the major. "M Troop's been cut to pieces; they're holding on, but it's an all night ride."

"Four troops," snapped Custer. "Four troops now and two in reserve to leave in an hour. Captain, will you send for my orderly? And, Major, I want you to take command of the reserve."

The captain strode off, Custer nodded to the major and turned away. His eyes took in Leach, standing at attention, went past him. He took two steps, then wheeled and his sharp eyes searched Leach's face.

"I know you. From where?"

"Thirty-second Missouri, sir!"

Custer's eyes squinted for a moment, then widened in astonishment. "Thirty-second Missouri! Good Lord, I remember now. You're the man—of course—you led the company that broke up Stuart's right wing ..." He snapped his fingers. "Captain Leach!"

"Private Leach, sir!"

The general took a step toward Leach. *"Private* Leach! That's ridiculous . . ."

"I only enlisted two days ago."

"You enlisted . . . as a private? Why the devil didn't you come to me . . . ? Wait a minute, I remember, I recall something else now." His sharp eyes again searched Leach's face. "There was some trouble . . . I was in St. Louis after the war and when I read about it, I sent you a note—"

"Yes sir!"

"Ah yes, I never forget a face or a name. It comes back to me." He shot a quick look over his shoulder. "There isn't time now, but . . . M Troop, aren't you? Of course! You're the man who brought word. Are you up to riding back with us?"

"Of course, sir!"

"Good. You'll ride with me." A smile flitted across his gaunt features. "Not like we did during the war, three thousand strong, but enough for any bunch of savages we're apt to meet. I guess they need to be reminded of the lesson I gave them on the Washita. . . . Here comes the orderly with the horses!"

A trooper, riding one horse and leading another, came up, saluted Custer. "Ready, sir!"

Custer returned the orderly's salute. "You'll stay here this time. Captain Leach will ride your mount."

The orderly dismounted, gave Leach a curious glance and handed him the reins of his horse.

Custer sprang into the saddle of his own mount. "You've told Mrs. Custer?"

"Yes, General."

"Good." He pointed across the parade ground. "What's molding up F troop? The men aren't even out of the barracks. Get over there and tell the commander I want his men in the saddle in five minutes."

The orderly ran off and Custer shook his head. "It's a good regiment, Captain Leach. I made it. I've given nine years to it."

"I know, sir."

A hundred yards to the left the band had assembled in front of its quarters. It struck up the regimental march,

56

"Garry Owen," and Leach, watching the general, saw the proud smile that came over his face.

Across the parade ground the troops were marching toward the stables. One was coming out, mounted, and started toward the front of the fort, at a brisk canter.

Five minutes later, four troops of the Seventh were swirling through the gates of Fort Lincoln, Custer, with Leach at his side, riding at the head. By sundown the battalion was five miles from the fort.

The Seventh Cavalry pushed westward through the night. It made periodic rest stops, but they were short. The horses were crowded to the limit of their endurance, but only a few men fell out along the way. The Seventh Cavalry was a good regiment; the men were the best, the mounts were well chosen and from frequent hard exercise had developed stamina.

Dawn found the regiment plodding along at a mile-eating pace. Leach, getting his bearings, discovered that they were already beyond the scene of the wagon train massacre.

"An hour, sir," he told the general.

Custer nodded. "We've made good time and the horses aren't in too bad shape. Although I'm afraid we won't be able to pursue them before afternoon." He sighed. "But the main thing's to save M Troop."

A skirmisher came galloping back. Custer spurred his horse out to meet him.

"We flushed a couple of Sioux, sir!" the skirmisher told him. "But they got away. Our horses weren't fast enough."

Custer scowled. "So they'll know we're coming!"

"I'm afraid so."

"We won't find a savage within five miles of M Troop, then."

And it turned out that way.

When they came in sight of the river, there were campfires still burning, but men of the Seventh were already on the river bank, waving their hats.

Only a few men, though. The rest were on the island. Twenty-four dead, twenty-nine wounded. Only eight men without a wound. One sergeant on his feet. Captain Hol-

57

terman in a coma, Lieutenant Gregson, conscious, but suffering from a head wound. And not a Sioux in sight.

But there were surgeons with the relief party and they were quickly among the wounded. Camp was pitched on the east shore of the river and in half an hour Major Comstock's reserve troops came up. They were followed only twenty minutes later by the missing K Troop, from the south.

Sergeant O'Hara was with K Troop.

Three days after M Troop was rescued, Leach was back at Fort Lincoln. Four troops of the Seventh were still out, but the others had returned to the fort, many of the men in ambulances. The squad rooms of M Troop barracks each had only a man or two in them. In Squad Room A there were only Leach and a private named Miller. Corporal Stockbridge had died on the island. Fiore and Potts were alive, but in the hospital, Potts having received a wound after Leach's departure—only a few minutes, in fact, before he himself was supposed to have attempted a break-through.

In the middle of the afternoon, a hospital orderly came into the Squad Room. "Private Leach!" he called out.

Leach raised himself from the bunk on which he was resting. "Yes?"

"Private Leach? Lieutenant Gregson sent me over from the hospital. You're to report to him. At once."

Leach got wearily to his feet, opened his locker and got out his blouse and cap. The hospital orderly had already left and Leach followed. In front of the barracks he was hailed by O'Hara, coming out of the orderly room.

"Here, Leach, where do you think you're going?"

"To the hospital."

"Guess again, Trooper. There are a million things around here—"

"Uh-uh," said Leach. "Not just yet. Orders. Lieutenant Gregson's sent for me."

"What for?"

Leach shrugged. "Ask him."

O'Hara stared at him. "Been complainin' to him, have you?"

"About what, Sergeant? That you followed me across the river, after we left the island, and tried to shoot me?"

"What the hell are you talking about?" O'Hara cried.

"You don't know?"

"You know damn well I don't. But if you're trying to pick a fight with me . . ."

"Not today, I'm still too tired. Besides"—Leach looked up the street—"the lieutenant wants me—right away . . . !"

He walked past the sergeant.

Standing on the veranda of the sutler's store was Molly Quade. She saw Leach when he was still fifty yards away and running down the short flight of stairs came to meet him.

"John!" she said. "You're back—and well!"

"You were worried?"

"Of course. When we heard how many had been . . ." A shudder ran through her and her hand came up involuntarily and gripped Leach's arm.

"O'Hara's back, too," he said.

She whipped her hand from his arm, stepped back. "O'Hara!" she exclaimed. "Do you think . . . ?" her face flooded with sudden color and she whirled and ran away from him.

Leach stood still, watched her disappear into her father's store, then drawing a deep breath he continued on to the hospital.

An orderly conducted him to Lieutenant Gregson's bed. The lieutenant was propped up, a couple of pillows behind his back. His head was swathed in bandages, but he was able to wink at Leach.

"A little rough, wasn't it, Leach?"

"A close one, sir!"

"I hope I never have a closer. Captain Holterman will be out of action for two or three months, I'm told, but I'll be up and back at the troop in a week. In the meantime"—he stopped and regarded Leach steadily—"the troop's yours . . ."

Leach blinked in astonishment. "Mine? I—I don't understand."

"As of today, you're first sergeant of M Troop. Replacing Sergeant Parker. A good man."

"First Sergeant," repeated Leach. "But there are other sergeants left, and corporals."

"You're going over them. Some men will be transferred from other troops, including some noncoms, no doubt, and there'll be replacements, but the first sergeant's job is yours—permanently."

Leach's eyes clouded. "I'm not sure that I want the rank, sir. I appreciate what you—"

"Sergeant!" exclaimed Gregson. "You're a soldier of the Seventh Cavalry. No man in the Seventh refuses to obey an order." Then he relaxed. "And this order comes from the top, Sergeant. The General. He was here a half hour ago, asked me what sort of a troop M Troop thought itself that it could keep a man with your background a private. . . ."

Ten minutes later, Leach turned in to M Troop barracks, but instead of Squad Room A this time, he headed for the orderly room.

O'Hara was sitting in the first sergeant's swivel chair, his feet up on the roll-top desk. A cruel smile twisted his lips as he saw Leach.

"So you came right back. Couldn't wait—"

"Get out of here," Leach snapped. "Get out of this room and stay out."

For an instant O'Hara stared at Leach. Then his boots hit the floor with a crash and he kicked back the swivel chair.

"What the hell are you talking about?" he cried.

"Pull yourself together, O'Hara," Leach said grimly. "This is going to hurt—but you, this time. I'm the new first sergeant of M Troop. Get that, O'Hara, I'm the top sergeant of this outfit!"

The blood drained from O'Hara's face. His mouth fell open and a groan came from his throat. "No," he whispered. "It can't be. It can't. . . ."

"But it *is*, O'Hara, and furthermore, until Lieutenant Gregson gets out of the hospital, I'm in complete command of this troop. Now, get out of here and think it over. . . ."

O'Hara reeled from the room.

Eleven

TEN men were transferred to M Troop the next day. They came from various troops, the men each troop commander thought he could most readily spare. A couple of Regular M Troopers, with only slight injuries, drifted back from the hospital and two or three additional came the following day. They trickled back all through the next week. A pair of recruits came to the fort from eastern recruiting offices and were assigned to M Troop. Gradually the troop regained its strength and First Sergeant Leach found his days full from his duties.

He saw O'Hara during the following week, but the man seemed to have lost his spirit. Most of the time he avoided Leach and when he did encounter him he avoided speaking. During that week, Leach had occasion to go several times to the sutler's store, but only once was Molly in the place and she was waiting on another soldier at the time.

The four troops of the Seventh returned from the plains; they had encountered no body of hostiles. As always, the Indians had dispersed before the determined pursuit of a large group of soldiers. Nothing was settled, but reports of isolated atrocities trickled into Bismarck. A small party of Sioux raided a ranch here, an emigrant at another place. Prospectors in the Black Hills disappeared; sometimes their mutilated remains were found, often not.

Three weeks from the date of the fight at Nelson's Island—named after the First Lieutenant of M Troop who had died there—Lieutenant Gregson returned to the troop. He came into the orderly room wearing the shoulder straps of a first lieutenant.

He made a tour of inspection with Leach and complimented him afterwards. "The troop's looking good again, Sergeant."

"We're still short twelve men, sir."

"We'll get them gradually; we've first call on the recruits coming in. I think I'd rather have them than the misfits that the other troop commanders would palm off on us in transfers. By the way, you've noticed that I've moved up a grade."

"I have, sir. Congratulations."

"Thank you. I'm still the only active officer in the troop, for Captain Holterman will be laid up another month or so. There's a second lieutenancy open. I talked to the skipper yesterday and we, that is, he, wondered if you cared to try the officers' examination . . . ?"

Leach hesitated. "Is that an order?"

"No. You can't order a man to become an officer in the Army. Only . . ." Lieutenant Gregson frowned. "I believe you could pass the scholastic examination without any trouble. You were a lawyer once—"

"Who told you that?" exclaimed Leach.

"As a matter of fact," the Lieutenant said slowly, "I know your story. The General that day at the hospital let something drop and I—I've had a lot of time in the hospital. I got hold of an old newspaper file . . ."

"I'd rather not talk about it, sir," Leach said bitterly.

"You mean it still bothers you . . . after nine years?" Lieutenant Gregson stared at Leach for a moment, then changed the subject abruptly, talking of troop matters. When he left a few minutes later, Leach went into the little bedroom off the orderly room that was the first sergeant's quarters and threw himself down upon his cot.

For a long time he lay there, staring sightlessly at the ceiling, as memories crowded in on him.

Nine years. Nine bitter, empty years. And the end was not yet in sight.

He rose heavily from the cot, went into the orderly room and stared out of the window upon the parade ground, where a cavalry troop was drilling.

Exclaiming softly he left the room and walking to the stables saddled his horse and rode it out of the fort, down to the ferry landing and across the river.

On the north bank of the river he put the horse into a brisk canter, in the direction of Bismarck, four miles away.

He rode into the town and tied his horse to a hitchrail a short distance from the railroad depot, in front of a saloon, which bore a huge sign across its false-fronted second story: *Dakota Palace.*

Leach ducked under the hitchrail and entered the saloon. It turned out to be a long, narrow room with a bar running down one entire side. About three feet of the back bar mirror was broken out.

Leach stepped up to the bar and pointed to a bottle of rye on the back bar.

The bartender picked up the bottle, held it in his fist and scowled at Leach. "How many drinks are you going to have here?"

"Does it matter?"

"It matters. A soldier come in here yesterday, had five drinks and broke that there mirror. You can have four drinks, that's all."

"Four'll be about all I can stand in this place," Leach retorted.

The bartender put the bottle down on the bar and watched Leach fill a small glass to the brim. "If you put your fingers around the glass," he said sarcastically, "you could get an extra half inch. No wonder your sutler's moving out, the way you soldiers do things."

Leach tossed off his whiskey without spilling a single drop and started pouring out a second glass. Halfway through the job, he looked at the bartender.

"What sutler's moving out?"

"Quade, who else?"

"Quade's leaving Fort Lincoln?"

"I just told he was. How come you don't know about it?"

"I've been busy." Leach filled up the glass, sipped at it slowly. "Why's he leaving?"

"How should I know? All I heard was that he sold his license and was pulling out for the Black Hills."

"The Black Hills!" exclaimed Leach. "With the Indians on the warpath?"

The bartender snorted. "I never heard of no Indians stoppin' a gold hunter. There's a town sprung up out there, Deadwood; she's a ripsnortin' place from all I heard."

"And have you heard of the new Indian law?" demanded Leach grimly. "Every Indian off the reservation after January thirty-first is declared a hostile. Have you any idea what that means?"

"No Indian law ever meant nothin'."

"This one means war; a full scale Indian war."

"Pah! A regiment of soldiers shoots three Indians and it's an Indian war. Like that crap last month. A hundred soldiers surrounded by eight Indians. The Battle of Nelson's Island! The trouble with you soldiers is you got to play everything up big. Make yourselves heroes."

"You don't like soldiers, I take it?" Leach asked ominously.

"You take it right. Come in here, spend forty cents, shoot off their mouths and break up—"

"Like this!" said Leach and, catching up the bottle of whiskey, hurled it at the head of the bartender. The man ducked frantically and the bottle missed him by the width of a sheet of paper. But it didn't miss the back bar mirror. It smashed virtually all that was left of the glass.

The bartender let out a howl that could have been heard at Fort Abraham Lincoln. Then he caught up a bung starter and started climbing over the bar.

Leach stepped back, waited for the man to clear the bar, then stepped forward and sent a smashing blow to the man's stomach. He followed through with a terrific uppercut that sent him reeling back against the bar.

He fell to the floor from there, but Leach didn't bother to watch him. He turned on his heel and headed for the door. He swung through and outside turned left. He walked fifty feet and entered another saloon.

The bartender here was a silent man and Leach had two drinks. Then the door bellied inward and the bartender from the Dakota Palace came in, followed by a lean, lank man who had a star on his vest.

"There he is, Marshal!" the bartender cried, pointing. "Broke a hundred dollar mirror, four bottles of my finest whiskey. Not to mention bustin' a chair over my head."

"That right, soldier?" asked the Marshal quietly.

64

"I broke a bottle of whiskey," Leach replied.

"What'd you wanna do that for?"

"He made some remarks about the Army that I didn't care for."

"He lies like hell!" howled the bartender. "He came into my place, drunk, lookin' for a fight. He practically wrecked the place, then he says he broke a bottle of whiskey. I want a hundred dollars, no less!"

"I'll pay you for the bottle of whiskey," Leach said. "The mirror was already broken."

"Well," said the Marshal mildly, "there seems to be a difference of opinion as to the amount of damage done. I guess we'd all better go see Judge Lipscomb and get it straightened out."

"I'll pay two dollars—for the whiskey," Leach said, doggedly. "I don't need a Judge to decide what I did."

"You're resistin' arrest?" The Marshal shook his head. "I hate to do this, but if I hafta, I hafta . . ."

His right hand went down, came up and a long-barreled Frontier Model was suddenly in his fist. Then the lanky Marshal stepped forward and with a movement that was pure lightning laid the barrel of the gun along the side of Leach's head.

Leach went down like a "good" Indian. He lay on the barroom floor, utterly motionless. "They just won't learn," the Marshal said sadly. He motioned to the bartender. "Grab hold of his legs. I got respect for Uncle Sam's uniform and I don't like to *drag* him over to the jailhouse."

Molly Quade, coming out of the Grand Leader Department Store, headed across the wooden sidewalk with her arms full of parcels. She had to stop as two men carrying a limp soldier crossed the sidewalk in front of her.

She grimaced in aversion at the sight, glanced idly into the unconscious soldier's face, then exclaimed, "What's wrong with him? Is he . . . ?"

"Naw," replied the Marshal laconically. "He ain't dead. I buffaloed him that's all."

"Why?"

"Drunk, disturbin' the peace. Nothin' serious, the Judge'll fine him twenty-five dollars and turn him loose."

"After I get paid for the damage he did to my place," snarled the bartender, who was carrying Leach's legs.

"Sure, sure," said the Marshal soothingly. "Well, come on, he's heavier'n he looks. Let's get him delivered."

The two men continued across the street with Leach, while Molly Quade stood on the sidewalk and watched them until they disappeared into the stout log cabin that was the Marshal's office and jail combined.

Twelve

ONE moment Leach was in utter oblivion; the next he was awake and aware of screaming pain in his head. He groaned and opened his eyes. He saw a dirty face, almost concealed by a matted beard, a foot over his own. He rolled to one side, sat up and, wincing back the shooting pains in his head, looked around.

He was lying on a bare canvas Army cot, in a room not more than ten by twelve feet in size. A single window, with iron bars across the outside of it, lit up the room.

There were two other canvas cots in the room, but only one other resident, the possessor of the dirty face, a derelict of indeterminate age. Snaggled teeth grinned at Leach.

"Right smart spell of sleep you had, mister. Four hours, almost."

Leach looked at the solid puncheon door that led to the front of the building. "This is the jail?"

"I guess you could call it that," said the vagabond. "Me, I prefer to call 'em calabooses. That Marshal fella's sure rough, ain't he?"

"He took me by surprise."

"Me, too. I wasn't doin' a thing, just mindin' my own business, then, wham. I wake up in here . . . I got thirty days, on account I didn't have twenty-five dollars to pay my fine. Eighteen days more to go . . . But I thought it was against the law to arrest a soldier. I remember my old pal, Herb Woodley, he was gonna join the Army on account of the law was after him for a small matter—"

Leach sprang up from the canvas cot and grabbed the hobo by the shoulder. "Did you say Herb Woodley?"

"Yeah, d'you know him?"

"If he's the Herb Woodley I know, he's dead," Leach said, shortly.

"I guess that's Herb, all right. The law got him in Chicago, two-three months back. Shot him down like a dog . . ."

Leach's fingers dug into the vagabond's shoulder. "How well did you know Herb Woodley?"

"Hey, you're hurtin' my shoulder," cried the hobo, trying to struggle out of Leach's savage grip.

Leach relaxed his grip on the man. "How long did you know him?"

"We bummed together for three or four years. We rode more freights, we was in more jails together—"

Leach shoved the man back. "When? I want dates. When did you first meet him—where . . . ?"

"It musta been about '71 that I first met him." The hobo suddenly backed away from Leach. "Say, you—you ain't the old pal of Herbie's what enlisted in the Army . . . ?"

"I was no friend of Herb Woodley's," snarled Leach. "I'm the man who killed him."

The hobo backing away was stopped by the log wall of the jail. His eyes were rolling in terror and his mouth twitched. "Y-you're the man followed Herb all those years, the fella he was always afraid of . . . ?"

"I'm the man," Leach said, moving toward his cellmate. "I followed Woodley for nine years and I killed him. But he died too quickly, he didn't suffer like I meant for him to suffer." He came up to the hobo and reached for him again.

The man slumped down to his knees, his arms thrown up to shield his face. "D-don't, mister, don't—don't kill me . . ."

"Then talk," Leach said ominously. "Tell me everything you know about Herb Woodley, or so help me—"

"Sure, sure," babbled the ragged man. "I'll tell you everything—everything you want to know. Like I told you, I bummed with him for three years and all that time Woodley was scared stiff. Of—of you . . . Said you were followin' him. He wouldn't stay any place more'n a day and sometimes he doubled back on his trail just to—just to see. He—he said you were a devil. Herbie said that, not me. Said you were going to kill him . . ."

"Did he ever tell you why?"

The hobo gulped. "No. I—mean he said he didn't do it. It was the other fellows. . . ."

"Who?" cried Leach. "Did he name them?"

"Some fellows he used to run with. I—I can't seem to remember their names now. Herb told me, but I—I—"

"Bligh," said Leach. "Bligh and Morrison . . ."

"That's them," exclaimed the hobo eagerly. "Bligh. Billy Bligh and—and Sam Morrison."

"Now, wait a minute before you go any further," Leach said. "I'll tell you the story straight and you can fill in the pieces." He drew a deep breath. "Nine years ago, Woodley, Bligh and Morrison held up a bank in Lexington, Missouri. As they came out, they got panicky and began shooting in all directions. A bullet hit a—a young lady . . . Helen Alderton. The bullet lodged in her spine and she was paralyzed for seven long months before death gave her relief. Woodley, Bligh and Morrison got away, but I saw one of them—I saw him from the window of Judge Alderton's law office, across from the bank. He rode right under me, and he looked up as he passed. I remembered his face and I—well, that's how I was able to follow him. I knew what he looked like. But unfortunately, I didn't see the faces of the other two men. Bligh and Morrison . . ."

"But you weren't a lawman," cried the hobo. "Why should *you* want to spend all that time runnin' them down . . . ?"

"I studied law under Judge Alderton," Leach said soberly. "He'd taken me into partnership with him and—and I was to marry his daughter, the day after she was shot."

"Gawd!" breathed the vagabond hoarsely.

A shudder ran through Leach and he became harsh, vindictive once more. "I got Woodley and I'm going to get Bligh and Morrison if it takes me the rest of my life. Now, what do you know about them?"

"Nothin', honest, Mister, I never saw neither one of them. Herb said they broke up not long after that—that bank job."

"Then how did you know that one of them enlisted in the Army?"

69

The hobo gulped. "I—a couple of years ago we was in St. Louis. We was campin' in a jungle down by the river and one day Herb come in from workin' the main stem and said he was goin' to enlist in the Army. Said he'd run into an old pal of his who'd enlisted four years ago and was a sergeant—"

"A sergeant?"

"Yeah. Woodley kept talkin' what a fine appearance he made. Big, strappin' sergeant. Woodley was all worked up, said the Army was the best place in the world for a man to hide. All the time he'd been runnin' and hidin' his old buddy, the sergeant, was livin' high and fine. Well, he went up and tried to enlist the next mornin' and ... and the Army wouldn't take him. Never saw a man so disappointed."

"This sergeant," Leach said carefully. "Did Woodley say what name he was using?"

"Yeah, but I can't seem to recall it. I never met him myself." He squinted in thought. "I seem to remember, though, that it was some kind of Irish name ..."

"O'Hara?" Leach suggested softly.

"O'Hara, O'Brien, somethin' like that. I'm not sure. It was a name you hear all the time. Couldda been O'Hara."

"Skip it for a moment. Now, think carefully. This soldier—whatever his name was—did you get the impression from Herb Woodley that *he* knew he was being hunted?"

"The sergeant?"

"Yes."

"Well, sure, it was him gave Woodley the idea that the Army was the best place for him to lose himself. The Indian country, he said, nobody in his right mind would go out there lookin' for somebody, with the Indians on the warpath all the time ..."

Leach whirled away from the hobo, headed for the door at the other side of the cell, but before he reached it he turned back.

"Is your being here in Bismarck an accident? Or ... did you come here for a reason?"

The tramp hesitated. "Well, it ain't exactly an accident, but I don't think I got a real reason, either. On'y ... well, before you ... I mean, before Herb died he talked about

70

comin' out here. He didn't say why, but I got to thinkin' about it and—well, things were pretty bad all summer. We had pretty hard times and Woodley sometimes talked about lookin' up an old friend and gettin' a stake from him . . ."

"O'Hara!"

"I dunno, I ain't so sure that was the name. But I do know that Woodley wanted to come out here to Bismarck, so I—well, after he was gone, what with the hard times and winter comin' on . . ."

"You thought you'd take over in Woodley's place. Find the sergeant and shake him down? But if you didn't know his name, how did you expect to find him?"

"Well, how many sergeants has Custer got?"

"You knew he was serving under Custer?"

"Yeah, sure, I told you, didn't I? Down in St. Louis, the sergeant was on recruitin' duty—gettin' fellas to enlist for General Custer. So I figured, I knew somethin' about this sergeant and I'd just kinda ask around and . . ."

But Leach was turning away from him. He stepped to the door and banged on it with his fist. "Marshal, open up!" he cried. "Open up. . . ."

Boots scraped the floor on the other side of the door and a calm voice retorted: "You prisoners don't stop makin' that racket, you're not goin' to get no supper and it's almost time."

"Marshal," exclaimed Leach. "This is Sergeant Leach. Open up, I want to talk to you . . ."

A key turned in the lock and the door was pushed inwards. Leach started to step through the door, but the lanky Marshal's hand fell to the butt of his six gun.

"Back up, soldier. I hate to buffalo a man twice in one day . . ."

"I've got to get out of here," said Leach. "You'd no right to arrest me in the first place."

"You know," the Marshal said laconically. "The soldiers always say that to me. I been thinkin' maybe it ain't legal to arrest soldiers—not even drunken soldiers that go around town smashin' up saloons . . ."

"I'm at the fort," Leach said. "First Sergeant Leach, of Troop M—"

"Leach of Troop M? Say, you're the lad who saved the troop at Nelson's Island."

"I'm the man who went for help, yes. Now, look, Marshal, it's important that I get back to the fort at once. You know where to find me. I'm not going to run away . . ."

"That you ain't, on account of you're stayin' right here until you pay—"

"All right," groaned Leach, "I'll pay for that damage. I only broke one bottle of whiskey, but I'll pay."

"Oh, that," said the Marshal. "I wasn't thinkin' of that. But this is a fee office, you know. Every time I arrest a man I get two dollars, fifty—"

Leach stared at the Marshal. "Two dollars and fifty cents . . . ?"

"Yep!"

"You mean, if I pay for that . . . ?"

"You can go!"

Leach thrust his hand savagely into his pocket, pulled out some bills and forced them into the Marshal's outstretched hand. Then he brushed past the man and hurtled into the Marshal's office, heading for the street door.

"Hey!" the Marshal called after him. "Here's your change . . . !"

But Leach didn't even hear him.

He tore out of the jail and started running across the street, toward the Dakota Palace Saloon, where his horse was still tied to the hitchrail.

He untied the horse and, vaulting into the saddle, put the animal into a gallop, out of Bismarck. Behind him, the sun was sinking below the horizon.

He kept the horse on the run all the way to the ferry and exclaimed in relief when he saw the scow on his side of the river. He drove the horse aboard and in a few minutes, sent it up the slope on the far side of the river, to the fort.

In the fort he rode swiftly to Troop M barracks and, dismounting, ran into the orderly room. He passed through it, into his quarters beyond and got his belt and revolver. Strapping the belt about his waist he plunged

72

out, and strode down a narrow hall to the rear, where several rooms were occupied by the sergeants of Troop M. He burst open the door of the first.

A sergeant, shaving, looked at him in surprise. "Where's O'Hara?"

There were two cots in the room, two wall lockers and chairs. The sergeant looked at the bunk opposite his own. "I don't know where he is, Sergeant."

"He's around somewhere?"

The sergeant hesitated. "No."

"What do you mean, no?" Leach cried. "This is where he sleeps, isn't it? He hasn't got leave and it's suppertime in a few minutes. Where would he be—the sutler's?"

"No, Sergeant. As a matter of fact, O'Hara didn't sleep here last night. And—well, his gun's gone and his personal belongings and—ninety-three dollars of my money that I kept in my locker."

Leach flinched. "He's gone over the hill?"

"That's what it looks like to me."

Leach began to swear. He strode to the wall locker behind O'Hara's bed and tore it open. It contained an extra uniform, but no shaving kit, no personal possessions. He slammed the door shut and whirled on the sergeant who was wiping the soap from his face.

"Why didn't you report this?"

"I did," replied the sergeant stiffly. "I went to the orderly room three or four hours ago, but you weren't there. I—I told Lieutenant Gregson. I couldn't report it last night, because I didn't know he'd skipped. I thought he might be staying in town overnight, but this afternoon, I needed some money and when I went to look for it, it wasn't there."

"Did O'Hara let drop any hint of his plans?"

"No, but he hasn't been the same since we got back from Nelson's Island. Frankly, Sergeant, he was pretty much put out when you were promoted over his head."

"That's to be expected. But did he ever talk about me, personally?"

"He didn't like you. Said the Seventh wasn't big enough for the two of you."

"Apparently it wasn't." Leach slammed out of the

73

room. Returning to his own quarters, he got a towel and some soap and went to the washroom at the rear of the barracks where he washed himself.

Finished, and noting the long bruise along his temple, put there by the Marshal of Bismarck, he returned to the orderly room. He had scarcely entered than the blast of a whistle from the mess hall announced supper. But Leach was in no mood for eating.

The barracks resounded to the noise of troopers hurrying to the mess hall, but Leach remained in his own quarters, until the din subsided. Then he put on his hat and left the barracks.

Thirteen

IT was dark outside, by this time, but there were lights in the sutler's store and Leach walked swiftly to it. He entered and found that the only occupants were the bartender and a corporal from Troop C, who had imbibed sufficient beer to make him unsteady.

"Hi, Sarge," he called. "Have a glassabeer."

"No, thanks."

"Oh, a corporal ain't good enough to drink with a top sergeant, huh? Well, lemme tell you, I was a sergeant myself once. Got busted and now I'm workin' my back. . . ."

Leach made an impatient gesture, as if brushing aside the corporal. He said to the man behind the bar: "Where's Quade?"

"Havin' his supper. Something I can get for you?"

"No. I want to see Quade himself."

Behind Leach, the voice of Molly Quade spoke: "About what?"

Leach turned quickly. Molly stood in the doorway that led to the living quarters of the Quades, behind the store. "I'd like to see your father," he said.

"I'm sure I could take care of your needs," Molly said coolly. "What is it you want—some smoking tobacco? Shaving soap . . . ?"

"I want to talk to him," Leach said harshly, "about Sergeant O'Hara!"

She seemed to flinch a little at his bluntness, but her answer came calmly enough. "Are you sure it's my father you want to talk to?"

"Yes." Leach stepped toward her. "Do you mind?"

She hesitated a moment then turned. "If you'll follow me. . . ."

He followed her through a small living room, into a combination kitchen and dining room. The sutler was

75

seated at a small table, eating the last of a piece of pie. He looked at Leach in surprise.

"Leach, isn't it? *Sergeant* Leach now, I believe."

"I want to ask you about O'Hara," Leach began, but the sutler cut him off short.

"You want to ask *me* about O'Hara? What do *I* know about him?"

"You were his best friend."

The sutler snorted. "I'm friends with hundreds of soldiers. Why wouldn't I be? I give them credit, sell them beer and listen to their troubles. . . ."

"O'Hara wasn't that kind of a friend."

"Who says he isn't?"

"I do. There was something between you two. . . ."

Quade pushed back his chair. "Now, look here, Leach, I don't know what the devil you're driving at—and what's all this *was*? You talk as if—"

"O'Hara's deserted!"

Quade stared at Leach in astonishment. "O'Hara, a deserter? What are you talking about?"

"Just that. He's deserted."

"I don't believe it!" exclaimed Molly Quade.

"It's true. He left yesterday." He added viciously, "Taking ninety-three dollars of another man's money with him."

Quade sprang to his feet. "Now, you're going too far, Leach, or whatever the devil your name is. I know O'Hara, yes, I know him well. And I know he's not the sort of man who'd take *anything* belonging to another man. All right, maybe he deserted, but if he did, he was driven to it. Yes, he told me—how you hounded him, gave him every dirty job—"

"O'Hara was a liar," Leach said remorselessly. "A liar, a thief . . . and a murderer . . .!"

"Get out of here!" roared Quade. "I won't have any man talking like that about a friend of mine, not in my house."

"Quade," said Leach, "did you ever hear of a man named Billy Bligh . . . or Sam Morrison?"

"No," thundered the sutler. "I never did. I don't know them and I don't know you." He snorted in derision.

"O'Hara a murderer! You should see the day you'll ever be one half the man that O'Hara was. You were jealous of him; by some underhanded conniving you got promoted over his head. You knew you didn't deserve it and you were afraid O'Hara'd get your rank, which he rightfully deserved. You persecuted the man until he couldn't stand it any longer. You forced him to throw away everything he'd gotten in seven years of hard work and you're not satisfied. You want to pursue him some more, put him into military prison . . ."

"If I find O'Hara," Leach said ominously, "he'll not go to prison. It'll be him or me. He tried to kill me a while ago and—"

"Rot!" snarled Quade. "I won't hear another word. Get out of here, before I call someone to throw you out. . . ."

Leach looked at the sutler, then at his daughter. Her face was white and drawn—and cold. He turned and strode to the door. There he stopped and faced the two in the room once more.

"You're pulling out of here, Quade," he said. "You'll probably be seeing O'Hara again. When you do, tell him for me, that I'll catch up with him and that this time I know who he is. Tell him that."

Then he walked out of the kitchen, through the living room and the store and out upon the parade ground.

In the darkness he walked back to Troop M barracks and discovered that his horse was still tied outside. He went up to the horse and was about to untie it, when he noticed that the light was on in the orderly room and that someone was seated at his desk.

He crossed to the barracks and entered. Lieutenant Gregson got up from Leach's desk. "Oh, here you are, Sergeant. You know about Sergeant O'Hara?"

Leach nodded. "I've just been inquiring about him down at the sutler's."

The lieutenant shook his head. "I can't understand it. We get desertions in the Seventh, although not as many as in some other regiments. But I've never known of a man in his second hitch deserting—and a sergeant, at that!"

"He took ninety-three dollars' of Sergeant Plennert's money."

"So Sergeant Plennert told me. It's hard to believe. Frankly, I never warmed up to O'Hara myself, but he wasn't a bad soldier. Rode the men a little too hard perhaps, yet"—the lieutenant's face clouded—"he went through the Indian lines with you at Nelson's Island and found the reserve battalion, you'll recall. If you hadn't been just a little faster at the time—"

"O'Hara went through the Indian lines with me," Leach said slowly. "And then he tried to kill me. . . ."

"What?" cried Lieutenant Gregson.

"I had a fight with O'Hara, coming out to Bismarck on the train, before I enlisted in the Seventh. I thought he held that against me, but—that wasn't the reason he tried to kill me. Lieutenant, when you returned from the hospital you said you'd learned my history, through the newspapers. . . . Well, O'Hara was one of the three men who—who killed my fiancée, Helen Alderton!"

"But how could you know that?" cried Gregson. "Those men were never identified . . ."

"I saw one of them," Leach said. "As they rode under the window of Judge Alderton's law office, one of them looked up. I saw his face. Of course I didn't know his name, then, but I checked back on every holdup that had been committed in the state by three men and I finally located Woodley's home, down in the Ozarks. I saw a picture of him there. They knew Morrison and Bligh, too; they had lived there for a while and associated with Woodley, but they were originally from somewhere else and there were no pictures of them. But it was enough that I knew Woodley. He would tell me about the others when I found him." Leach's face twisted. "I followed Woodley. I followed him for nine years. Nine long years, Lieutenant. I devoted every single minute of every day to just that one task . . . I—I caught up with him last summer."

"And . . . ?"

"I killed him. There were extenuating circumstances: Woodley'd become a common tramp and sneak thief. I'd followed him to Chicago and then lost him. By sheer accident I was on the scene when he tried to pick someone's pocket. There was a hue and cry and I got into the chase.

I got to Woodley first and I shot him—with his own gun. Before he died he let it out that his old companions, or at least one of them, were serving in the United States Cavalry. . . ."

"And that's why you enlisted in the Seventh?"

"Yes."

Gregson's face grew dark in sudden anger. "Damn it, Leach, I don't like it. The Army's no place for private feuds."

"It isn't exactly a private feud. O'Hara's a robber, a fugitive from justice—and a murderer!"

"Just the same, I'm disappointed in *you*, Leach. You're in the Army under false pretenses. You didn't enlist to become a soldier. You got in to find a man . . . and kill him."

"I'll kill O'Hara," Leach said evenly, "I'll kill him as he killed the woman I loved—and as he'll try to kill me. As he's already tried. I'll shoot him down like a mad dog."

Lieutenant Gregson banged his fist on Leach's desk. "You'll face a firing squad if you do, Leach. I'll see to it myself. I won't—the Army won't—stand for anything like that, no matter what your provocation. If you've any proof that O'Hara's done what you say he has—that he's the man who did those things, you can turn the information over to the civilian authorities. They'll get O'Hara from the Army, through legal means."

Lieutenant Gregson broke off and scowled at Leach for a moment. "Dammit, Sergeant, why did you have to tell me these things?"

"Why'd *you* pry into my private affairs?" Leach flared back.

Gregson smacked his right fist into his left hand. "I'm still the acting commander of this troop. In view of what you've just told me, I don't see how I can keep you on as first sergeant."

"I didn't ask for the stripes."

"Now, don't try throwing anything like that in my face, Leach. I won't have it. You rated your chevrons. With your service record and your performance at Nelson's Island you deserved the promotion. And I don't mind say-

79

ing that you've done a fine job as first sergeant, up to now. It's just this—this personal mess of yours. . . ." He suddenly stopped and looked sharply at Leach. "What are your intentions? Are you going after O'Hara? Are you also going to desert?"

"I—I hadn't thought of it."

"You're an old soldier, Leach. No matter what your private reasons, you wouldn't desert from the Army in time of war . . ."

"We're not at war."

"If we aren't, I don't know what war is," retorted the lieutenant. "All right, it's an undeclared war, but it's still a war. The Indian Reservation Law made it one. You're not the sort of a man who'd desert in the face of the enemy. All right, Sergeant, get your gear together. You ride in a half hour."

"Where to?"

The lieutenant chuckled grimly. "I came down here this evening to tell you that we've been ordered to supply a half troop to serve as escort for a wagon train. I told Sergeant Plennert, in your absence, that he'd go in command. But there's nothing in regulations says I can't send the top sergeant. So you'll go and Plennert will remain here, as acting first sergeant. You keep your rank, Sergeant, but you're on active duty as of this minute."

Leach looked at the lieutenant for a long moment. "Where's the wagon train headed for?"

"The Black Hills, a place called Deadwood. The government's withdrawn its ban on emigrants and we've got to protect the fools who insist on going into country like that." He chuckled again. "You'll see action, Leach, and if you think it isn't a war we'll be having out here, you'll wonder what peace is like. . . ."

He stopped as Sergeant Plennert stepped into the orderly room and saluted.

"The detachment is ready to fall in, sir," the sergeant announced.

"Good. But I've made a change, Sergeant. You'll remain here—as acting first sergeant. Sergeant Leach takes your place as leader of the detachment."

Sergeant Plennert's face remained impassive. "Very good, sir."

He saluted again and, about-facing, left the orderly room.

"I'll give you a half hour, Sergeant," Gregson said to Leach. "The wagon train's camped five miles west of Bismarck. You'll join it this evening and be ready to move out with them at dawn."

"I'll be ready in five minutes," Leach said.

He strode into his sleeping quarters and quickly assembled his gear. A whistle blasted somewhere in the barracks as he finished packing and when he came out, men were pouring out of the barracks onto the parade ground.

Leach joined the men there, called them to attention and got the reports of three corporals. Not counting himself, there were thirty-two men in the detachment, a little more than half the strength of Troop M.

Mounting his own horse, Leach marched the men to the stables and in a few minutes the detachment was mounted and ready to leave the fort.

Lieutenant Gregson came out of the darkness then and stepped up to Leach's horse. "I'm sorry I had to talk that way to you, Leach," he said, quietly. "But I happen to be a soldier. The Army's first with me. It'll always be."

"I understand, sir."

"I expect you back here."

"I'll be back."

"Good." Gregson held out his hand. "Good luck."

Instead of taking the hand, Leach saluted. "Thank you, sir." He half turned in his saddle. "Troop, attention! Forward, ho!"

In columns of twos, with Leach at the head, the detachment rode out of Fort Abraham Lincoln. Some of the men would never see it again. Too many of them.

Fourteen

IT was a bitterly cold morning, when Leach, sipping coffee beside a tiny fire, was approached by the leader of the wagon train, a huge, black-bearded man of about forty-five.

"You in charge of these soldiers?"

"Yes."

"I'm Kelso, captain of the wagon train. We're ready to pull out."

"Go ahead."

Kelso looked sneeringly around at the several fires over which the troopers were having their breakfasts. "Your men ain't ready yet."

"We'll catch up."

Kelso scowled. "I thought you soldiers were supposed to get up early."

"It was after midnight when we got in last night," Leach retorted. "There was no point in rousing them out at four in the morning. We're only five miles from Bismarck and there's no danger for you. So start out and we'll be up with you before you've gone a mile."

"I got sixty-five people in this train," Kelso said, "More'n half of them women and children. It's your job to protect them."

"We'll do our job."

"That means you gotta keep close to us all the time. It's a long way to Deadwood and there'll be snow any day. So we gotta start early in the morning and travel late. If your army figures to have its breakfast in bed every morning . . ."

Leach got to his feet. "Kelso, let's have an understanding right at the start. You're captain of the wagon train. Fine. Well, I'm in command of these troopers. I'll give them their orders and make the decisions for them. You do the same for your wagon train."

Kelso glowered at Leach then suddenly turned on his heel and walked back to the wagon train. Leach heard him yelling orders. He heard, too, the cracking of whips and then saw the lead wagons start off.

Leach drained the last of his coffee, washed out his tin cup, and spoke to one of the corporals. "Get the men ready."

The corporals began issuing orders and in ten minutes the troop was ready for the saddle. The last wagon of the train was less than a hundred yards distant.

"Mount," Leach ordered.

The troopers swung into saddles and in a moment the detachment was trotting after the wagon train. As he passed each wagon Leach counted it and when he reached the head of the train discovered that there were twenty-four wagons. A sizable train.

Reaching the head of the train, Leach summoned the corporals and through them got eight men with plains experience. He sent them out as skirmishers, two to the front, two to the left, two to the right, and two to fall behind the train and remain at a comfortable distance, to prevent a surprise attack from the rear.

The wagons made good time during the morning and, when the noon halt was called, had traveled ten miles. They covered another eight or nine miles in the afternoon and when camp was pitched they were almost twenty-five miles from Bismarck and quite a few miles beyond the last settler's cabin.

Leach now had his second altercation with Kelso, the captain of the wagon train. Kelso called on him. "You're puttin' out enough sentries, ain't you?" he demanded.

"I'm putting out sentries, yes," replied Leach. "But so are you. I haven't enough men to guard this large camp properly, every night."

"You've got thirty-two soldiers," blustered Kelso. "More'n we have men in the train."

"I've got to keep eight skirmishers out every day," Leach said. "More, as we get into the Indian country. I can't expect those men to be alert if they have to stand guard at night. And I can't have more than half of my remaining force on guard each night. I think it's up to you to put out a few men at night, at least to watch your live-stock."

"We'll do nothin' of the kind," Kelso declared. "You got orders to do the guardin' and you're going to. Our men have to drive their wagons durin' the day and they can't stand up all night, doin' your work."

"Your men can sleep in the wagons during the day, while their wives drive. We haven't got any wagons. I'll furnish ten men for guard duty every night, five of them four hours on, four off. That's the best I can do."

"We'll see about that," Kelso snarled and walked back to the wagons.

Later, however, a quiet man from the wagon train called on Leach. "Ten troopers for guard duty will be fine," he said. "We'll guard our own livestock."

"Good," said Leach. "My men won't be worth a damn, if I don't keep them in condition."

"I understand," said the emigrant, shaking his head. "Kelso knows the country, which is the only reason we elected him captain, but he's got a hatred for the Army that none of us like. If he gets too obstreperous we'll have to elect us a new captain."

Leach himself posted the guards that night. Following the custom of '49 the wagons were formed in a circle, tongue to tail and only two civilian guards were posted inside the circle. But the horse herd and the numerous head of beef that the emigrants were taking along with them had to graze during the night and they were placed inside of large rope corrals, flimsy enclosures at best. Knowing the tendency of the Indians to stampede the horses before an attack, Leach felt that a substantial guard should be posted among the animals and he saw that a half dozen of the emigrants were detailed for the assignment.

The cavalry horses were kept separate from the emi-grant's animals. They were trained and accustomed to the picket line and Leach put only two troopers with them, since the soldiers' camp was near by. The other three sentries he posted at a considerable distance from the camp, at the points of a large triangle that took in the entire en-campment.

All went well that night, however, and the next day the

wagon train got an early start and clipped off an easy twenty miles. Indian smoke signals were seen during the day and the campsite was carefully chosen.

Fires were built and the odors of cooking were soon wafted about. Leach, sitting down to his own meager rations, was roused by a sudden shout from the wagon train near by. He got to his feet and looking eastward saw a large Conestoga wagon coming toward the camp at a good pace.

"I didn't know there were any stragglers today," he said to a trooper.

"There weren't; this is some damn fool travelin' alone."

Leach walked toward the camp. The approaching wagon was close by that time and he suddenly exclaimed softly. There were two people on the seat of the wagon: Sam Quade, the sutler of Fort Lincoln, and his daughter, Molly.

As the wagon came to a stop it was surrounded by a number of the emigrants. "I'd like to join your train," Quade announced to the assemblage. "I traveled most of last night to catch up with you."

"You're the sutler from Fort Lincoln, ain't you?" Kelso asked.

"Yes. I sold my license several days ago. I wasn't planning to leave for Deadwood for a few days, but when I heard that this would probably be the last train leaving before winter, I packed up in a hurry. Left Bismarck at noon yesterday."

"You can ride with us," said Kelso, "but we made up a set of rules you got to stick to. We got a cavalry escort and we shouldn't ought to have any trouble."

Leach stepped forward. Quade exclaimed when he recognized Leach. "You're in charge of the soldiers?"

"Yes."

"If I'd known that I think I'd have stayed in Bismarck."

The wagon train captain moved toward Quade. "What's the matter with the sergeant?"

"We just don't happen to be friends," Quade replied.

Kelso showed his teeth in a wolfish grin. "Mister," he said, "you're welcome with us."

85

Leach walked back to the troopers' camp, finished his frugal supper, and then went out to check up on the sentries. "You saw those smoke signals today," he cautioned one of the men.

The soldier nodded. "We can't be very far from Nelson's Island."

"About twenty miles. We'll miss it by a dozen miles tomorrow, for we're headed in a more southerly direction, but there'll be Indians from here on, so I don't have to warn you about falling asleep."

Leach returned to the cavalry camp and rolled himself in his blankets, hoping for a couple of hours sleep in the early evening, as he expected to get up several times during the night. But sleep would not come and after awhile he got up and started in the direction of the emigrants' livestock herd.

A shadowy figure detached itself from the circle of wagons and came toward him. A voice that Leach knew called to him: "John! John Leach. . . ."

Leach stopped and Molly Quade came up to him. She stopped three feet away and he could just barely make out her features in the reflected light from the campfires.

"I'm sorry, John," she said. "I—I had to tell you."

"Sorry that I'm with the wagon train?" he asked.

She exclaimed softly. "Don't! You know very well what I mean."

Leach was silent for a moment. Then he said tonelessly: "Yes, I know what you mean and—and *I'm* sorry . . . sorry that there isn't anything in me, except the will to kill two men."

She recoiled. "That's all that your life means—killing?"

"It's all that I've lived for these past nine years."

"That's ridiculous, John," she cried. "I—I've asked about you at the fort. You were an officer during the war; your record was brilliant. General Custer himself cited you and then you threw it all away for this mad . . . what is it, vengeance? How could any wrong anyone did mean so much to you?"

Leach was silent and Molly took a step closer to him. "Tell me, John, I—I've *got* to know. . . ."

"There was a girl," Leach said, barely above a whisper.

86

"We were to be married and then—the day before—she was shot. Oh, she wasn't killed. No, she wasn't that lucky. The bullet paralyzed her and for seven months she lay in bed, unable to move a muscle. I watched her die, slowly, day by day. . . ."

"How horrible!" exclaimed Molly, shivering.

"Maybe I died then, too," Leach said. "At least a part of me, the part that made life worth living. I haven't had it in me all these years. All I've had is, all right, you called it vengeance, I call it retribution. It's the only thing that keeps me going. They killed her, those men, and I'll kill them. There were three and there are still two. . . . O'Hara and the other man whose name I'll get when I finally face O'Hara for the last time."

"And then?" Molly Quade asked. "What then, John Leach, after you've played God twice more? What, then?"

"I don't know," Leach replied harshly. "Maybe one of them will get me, too. But it'll be the last one. It's *got* to be."

"And what if you don't die? What if you've got to go on living after you've kil—after you've fulfilled your mission? Can you go back and find yourself again? Those lost years."

Leach was moved; for the first time in a long, long while, he knew an emotion other than the one that had so filled his years. "I don't know," he said desperately. "I don't know."

Molly moved away, back toward the circle of wagons. Leach remained where he was, his entire body quivering. He thought that Molly had gone altogether, but then she spoke once more, from a distance of a dozen feet.

"When you know, John, find me—and tell me."

Then she was gone.

Fifteen

IN the middle of the next morning, a trooper came galloping back to the wagon train. Leach, at the head of the cavalry detachment, rode out to meet him.

"Indians," the trooper reported. "Me and Osborne flushed a party of them. Six or seven, in war paint."

"Where are they?"

"They went skedaddling when they saw us."

"They saw just the two of you and ran?"

"That's right, Sergeant. But I thought I'd better ride back and tell you."

Leach nodded. "Go back to Osborne, but keep separated, at least a hundred feet. That war party didn't run from you because they were afraid."

"I didn't think so."

"If you sight them again, fire a shot and if they attack you, don't try to fight them off. Fall back. But remember, keep a safe distance from Osborne, so that you can't both be jumped at one time. Keep in sight of each other, though, and the minute one of you doesn't see the other, let go with your gun."

"Right, Sergeant."

The trooper rode off.

A horse came galloping up from the wagon train. Leach, turning in the saddle, saw Kelso, the captain of the wagon train, bearing down on him.

"What's up?" Kelso asked.

"The point sighted Indians," Leach replied. "Just a half dozen. Not enough to be alarmed."

"Where there's one redskin, you'll find another."

"True, but we've got to expect to see Indians. After all, we're in the heart of their country. I'd be more uneasy if I didn't see any."

Kelso pointed suddenly to the west. "Look, smoke

signals! That bunch your men saw is signaling to another bunch."

Leach studied the puffs of smoke that were floating in the sky. Even as he looked, answering puffs went up to the south and west. He shook his head.

"All right, face it," he snapped at Kelso. "You expected you might have to fight when you started out on this trip."

"We'll never make it," Kelso declared. "It's another two hundred miles, a good ten-twelve days. It's suicide to go ahead. You call in your soldiers, we're going back."

He whirled his horse and sent it galloping back to the wagon train.

Leach raised his arm in a signal for the troop to halt. "You can dismount," he said to the soldiers, "but remain on the alert."

Leach himself remained in the saddle. The wagon train had come to a halt and a large group of the emigrants assembled near the lead wagon.

Leach waited ten minutes, then rode down to the group.

"What's the decision?" he asked.

"We haven't arrived at one," Kelso snapped. "Some of these damn fools insist on going ahead."

"I'm going," one of the men declared. "We knew in Bismarck that the Indians were hostile. I don't see that the situation has changed any.'"

"That goes for me, too," another emigrant said. "I expected to have to kill a few Indians and I'm ready for a fight."

"You've never fought Indians," Kelso declared. "You ain't got any idee what it's like. They keep comin' and comin' at you. You kill one and two of them jump up and take his place."

"They won't attack us," a third emigrant put in. "We're too strong. When they see the soldiers they'll keep their distance."

"What do you think, Sergeant?" another man asked. "Will they attack us?"

Leach shrugged. "I don't know. They might attack, if there's a big enough war party in the neighborhood. But a wagon train's a pretty formidable thing to beat, if it's prepared for a battle. You've got cover and the Indians are in the open."

"Let's put it to a vote," a man exclaimed. "Those who want to go ahead can go and the others can turn back."

"No," said Leach. "My duty's to protect you and I can't break up my force and try to protect two groups. Neither one would be strong enough to fight off any determined attack. I don't care what your decision is; you can go back if you want to or you can go ahead, but you've all got to go together."

"Vote!"

"Vote on it!"

Several minutes more were taken up by acrimonious discussion but then the emigrants finally settled on the vote. Kelso threw a rope on the grass. "All those in favor of going ahead, step over the rope. Those who want to turn back to Bismarck stay on this side."

He folded his arms to indicate that he was staying right where he was.

Kelso lost. More than two-thirds of the emigrants stepped across the rope.

The decision was scarcely arrived at than a gun banged somewhere off to the left. Leach whipped his horse about, shot a quick glance over the troop of cavalry, and beyond saw both of the left wing skirmishers galloping back toward the wagon train.

"Get ready to fight," Leach shouted over his shoulder, as he put the spurs to his mount.

The animal leaped forward and Leach rode swiftly out to meet the two skirmishers. They were shouting at him before he could distinguish their words and he pulled up his horse ready to turn and run with them.

Then their words came: "Sioux! A million of 'em . . . !"

Leach saw them then, just topping a low knoll less than a mile away. He whipped out his Colt and fired three times into the air, signal for the other skirmishers to come in to the main troop body.

The two skirmishers came tearing up and Leach turned with them and rejoined the troop. From there, Leach studied the charging Indians. They were strung out along

90

the prairie, a good sixty or seventy, perhaps more. And off to the right, from the west, came another band. The second group was at a little further distance, however.

Leach made a quick decision. "Get the horses into the wagon circle," he ordered the troop. "It's going to be a tough fight and we want as many of them spared as possible."

The emigrants were already forming a circle of wagons. It would be completed in a minute of two—but that would not be soon enough. The first detachment of Indians would hit them before that time.

Leach had to stop the Indians, at least long enough for the emigrants to complete their circle. Galloping the troop back to the emigrants' wagons, he brought them to a quick halt and yelled out:

"Dismount! Horse holders take the mounts and lead them into the circle, and then return here at once ... Troop attention!"

Every fourth man caught the reins of three horses in addition to his own, according to the cavalry drill, and the other troopers quickly formed a double rank, facing the first group of charging Indians, now less than a half mile distant.

"Prepare to fight on foot," Leach ordered. "At intervals, take distance. Move!"

As if they were on the parade grounds the double rank melted into a single line, each man ten feet from the next one.

"Down!" roared Leach.

The men dropped to the ground, carbines thrust out before them. Leach went down to his knees at the far right of the line, facing the men.

"Hold your fire until I give the order," Leach shouted, remembering the devastation created in a similar situation at Nelson's Island.

The Indians were swooping down in a wide half circle that would catch the wagon train in a pincers. Leach, swiveling, saw the second horde of Indians, now about a mile distant. They would hit from thirty to sixty seconds after the first wave. That was better than a simultaneous attack, but still, if Leach's men failed to stop the first attack quickly enough, it could be disastrous not only to the soldiers, but the emigrants.

As Leach watched, the two skirmishers from the rear pounded up. He ordered them to drive their horses into the enclosure. As they charged through, the eight troopers who had taken the horses inside came pouring out.

Leach ordered them to take up a kneeling position behind his first line of prone men and instructed a corporal to watch for the other skirmishers and as they came up to join the kneeling row. The circle of wagons he saw was now complete, but the emigrants were by no means ready to join in the fight. They were dashing about, taking care of the women and children, setting up kegs and boxes for shelter. The brunt of the first attack would fall upon the cavalrymen.

And now Leach could no longer take his eyes from the advancing Indians. They were three hundred yards distant, already firing irregularly. And whooping.

Two hundred yards. A hundred.

"Get ready!" Leach shouted above the din and thrust his own revolver out.

"Fire!"

A sheet of flame and thunder rolled from the line of troopers stretched out on the grassy sod.

The result of the volley was fearful. Charging horses turned complete somersaults, throwing their riders and in some cases crushing them with their heavy carcasses. Other Indians, torn from the backs of their mounts, were trampled by horses. But those Indians not hit by the blast of death were coming at such terrific speed that they could not pull up short in front of the soldiers. The second volley from the smaller group of soldiers in the second line brought down several Indians. And then the men on the ground, having levered fresh cartridges into chambers, let go with another round, almost in the faces of the charging Indians and horses.

Almost two-thirds of that first wave of Indians went down, half their horses were dead or wounded. Panic seized the survivors of the charge and in their mad efforts to get away, they swarmed in every direction. The troops came up from the ground and blasted away individually at them.

Leach, roaring at the top of his lungs to be heard over the tremendous din, finally swerved the soldiers.

"The right," he cried, "face to the right."

And only just in time. The second wave of Indians, coming from the other direction, was already within a hundred yards. Their speed was diminishing, however, for they had noted the havoc of their tribesmen's charge.

"Load!" roared Leach. "Fire at will!"

The Indian charge broke, rather it suddenly swerved from a head-on charge to a flanking one, the Indians galloping alongside the soldiers and the encircled wagon train.

They offered beautiful targets and the soldiers picked off men with a vengeance. The Indians fired, too, but, notoriously bad marksmen, their aim was not improved by being on horseback.

A dozen Indians went down from the second wave and then the Indians were out of rifle range. Circling, they went off to the left and mingled with the survivors of the first disastrous charge.

Leach made a quick survey of his men. Two were down, one dead, the other badly wounded. Three of those standing had suffered minor wounds. But those were the only casualties. The Indians ... keeping his distance from them, Leach counted more than thirty, dead or wounded on the ground and there were undoubtedly other wounded who had been able to ride or run off.

A half dozen emigrants, rifles ready, came plunging out of the wagon circle.

"Gawd!" cried one of them as he surveyed the carnage. "You practically wiped them out."

Leach kept his eyes on the Indians who had assembled a quarter of a mile away. As nearly as he could judge there were sixty or seventy survivors.

The train captain, Kelso, came running up. He saw one of the Indians on the ground, trying to crawl away, threw up his gun and fired. The Indian dropped.

"That baby'll never scalp anyone," he exulted.

"You'll shoot no more wounded," Leach snapped.

"What the hell you talkin' about?" Kelso snarled. "We're goin' out there and make sure every damn one of them is dead. It's what they'd do to us, if it was the other way around. And they'd do more'n that."

"But *you* won't," Leach said. "What you'll do is get the wagons rolling again. The Indians want their dead and wounded. They've had enough; there won't be another attack."

Kelso started to bluster, but a couple of the emigrants silenced him. "That's enough, Kelso," one of them declared. "After what the sergeant's done here with his soldiers, he can tell us anything he wants and we'll do it."

To be on the safe side, however, Leach waited ten minutes. Then, when it was plain that the Indians were not going to attack again, the wagon train was put into motion.

It traveled only a mile when Leach called it to a halt and had it prepared for an attack. Then he rode back to the battlefield, with a half dozen men. He found only dead horses. All the Indian dead and wounded were gone. And so were the live Indians.

Leach led his detachment back to the emigrant train and it was once more put into motion, traveling until sundown before halting for the night.

A strong guard was posted that night, but the camp was unmolested. Indians were sighted the next day, but only small groups who kept their distance. A raid on the horse herd by a half dozen young bucks was beaten off during the night and that was the last shot that was fired for the rest of the journey to Deadwood.

Sixteen

NINE days later, after a forced march, the emigrant train entered the canyon in which the Black Hills mining town was located.

Leach picked a site at the edge of town and had his men pitch camp. Before the campfires were lighted, a man from the Wells Fargo Agency sought out Leach.

"Got a letter here for you," he said. "Came in on the stage from Yankton today."

Leach opened the letter and discovered that it was an order from Lieutenant Gregson of M Troop, directing him to establish an outpost accessible to Deadwood for the purpose of maintaining military protection for the inhabitants of Deadwood and vicinity. Lieutenant Brown would arrive within a few days to assume command.

Leach swore softly when he read the orders. He had expected to start back to Bismarck the following morning.

He read the order to the troopers. Grumbling was prompt and unanimous. None of the men relished the idea of remaining in Deadwood throughout the winter. Bismarck was bad enough when the icy winds howled over the Dakota prairies, but it had a railroad. Furloughs could be obtained. And there was a large Army fort at Bismarck with entertainment, recreation. That could be obtained at Deadwood, true, but it was a boom mining camp and the pay of a soldier would provide about one evening's entertainment a month.

Leach listened to the complaining but made no comment himself. A light snow had already fallen that day and the Black Hills would soon be in the grip of winter. The search for O'Hara had received a setback and if he were not relieved of command soon it might well be spring before he could resume it. But then, he had already been nine years on the trail. One more would not matter too much.

Leach had a frugal supper at the camp, then walked into the town. He turned in at one of the general stores and arranged for the purchase of a number of axes and saws, then from there proceeded to the office of the town marshal, who turned out to be a notorious gunfighter from Kansas, recently turned marshal. His name was Selby and he was a youthful, round-faced man with a cherubic face.

"You're the man just brought in the emigrant train," he said to Leach. "Had a rather rough time of it, I hear."

"It could have been worse."

The marshal grinned wickedly. "You soldiers going to hang around here for a while?"

"I have orders to establish a barracks."

"Good enough, but I don't mind telling you right now that soldiers are no better than anyone else. They get drunk and start fights, I'll lock 'em up as fast as anybody."

"You can argue that point with Lieutenant Brown, who'll be in command. He'll be here in a few days." Leach nodded toward the reward posters tacked to the wall. "Been a lawman long?"

"Who, me? I'm Dick Selby. Mean to say you've never heard of me?"

"The name sounds familiar."

The marshal snorted. "I should hope it does." He shrugged. "This is the first time I've worn tin. They couldn't get anybody else to take the job, so I said I wouldn't mind taking a crack at it. Not a bad idea. Pays well."

"It's a fee office?"

"Partly. A hundred a month and two dollars for every arrest. But I got a guarantee of two hundred a month, which ain't bad money these days."

Leach, thinking of his own salary, nodded agreement. "I suppose, this being a boom town and people coming in all the time, you don't get to know many of them."

Selby shrugged. "They come and go all the time, but the last couple of weeks they've thinned down pretty much. Nobody wants to get caught in the snow—not with

96

a million Indians around, lookin' for scalps. What'd you have in mind?"

"Why, I was wondering if you happened to know a man who might have come this way during the past week or so. Big, strapping fellow, about thirty-six, thirty-seven—"

"Deserter?"

"Well, yes."

"A sergeant, maybe?"

Leach's eyes narrowed. "He's been here?"

"I missed on him," said Selby. "It's fifty dollars they pay for deserters, isn't it?"

Leach made an impatient gesture. "When was he here?"

Selby stepped to the door, opened it. "Come along."

Leach followed the marshal out of the office and across the street to a log cabin store, which bore a sign: "The Golden Emporium."

Selby pointed to the window. "See what I mean?"

In the window, occupying the center position and surrounded by various other types of clothing, was a complete cavalryman's uniform. Sergeant's chevrons and a hash mark were on the sleeve of the blouse.

"Otto put it in the window yesterday morning," Selby said.

Leach stepped to the door of the store and, opening it, entered. Selby followed.

A balding, heavy-set man behind a counter was trying to sell a Prince Albert to a buckskin-clad, bearded man. "Otto," called Selby, from just inside the door, "come here."

"Just a minute, Sheriff," replied Otto. "I got a customer."

"No, you ain't," retorted the man in buckskins. "I said I wanted some store clothes, but damned if I'll wear one of them long-tailed preacher's coats."

"Preacher, nothing," the storekeeper exclaimed. "I bought this Prince Albert from a whiskey salesman who drew to an inside straight. In St. Louis and Chicago, bankers wear coats like this—"

"Otto!" called Selby. "I said, come here."

Otto shot a nervous glance at the marshal, then looked quickly back at his reluctant customer. He hesitated, then, licking his lips, said to the buckskin wearer: "Don't go 'way. I'll make you a nice price on this garment." He came quickly toward Selby and Leach. "Yes, Sheriff, what can I do for you?"

"That soldier suit in the window, Otto," the marshal began.

Otto clapped his hand to his forehead. "More trouble, now?"

"No trouble," said Leach. "Of course you're selling government property—"

"No, no, I bought it from a discharged soldier."

"A deserter."

"Ah, no, he was discharged. Look on the suit—it's got one of them little stripes on the sleeve that means he's finished one enlistment, already . . ."

"A hash mark," Leach said. "Yes, he was in his second enlistment. But he didn't finish it. He deserted."

The proprietor's eyes threatened to bulge from his forehead. "All right, I take the loss; I don't want no trouble with the Army. Or the government. I am out six dollars. You take the suit and we call it quits. Yes?"

"I'm not interested in the uniform. I want the man," Leach said.

"Sure, sure, but I don't know where he is. I never saw him before. He came in here the night before last and we made this here deal. I allowed him three, I mean six dollars on the uniform against a fine Prince Albert coat and the best broadcloth trousers you ever saw. Scarcely worn."

"What color?"

"Black. Well, kinda black, you know that dark grey pattern, with a darker stripe in it. I charged him only two dollars for the trousers. Eight dollars, I mean, ten dollars for the coat. And only a dollar for the hat. An excellent derby, that fitted him like as if it was custom made."

"Prince Albert, dark broadcloth pants, derby hat," Leach enumerated. "What else?"

"What else would he wear with that? A fine broadcloth shirt—"

"White?"

"Naturally. And a grey cravat and stiff collar."

"Reg'lar gambler's layout," observed Selby, the marshal.

"That's it!" exclaimed Otto eagerly. "Now you mention it, sure. I sold him a derringer, a fine double-barreled little gun you could hide in the palm of your hand. Like the gamblers carry."

"Sounds like your man's going into business," Selby said to Leach. "Card business."

"He's still got his Colt and a Spencer carbine," Leach replied. "And a horse belonging to the United States Government."

"All of which he needs, if he's traveling on."

"Where would you travel from here?"

"Me?"

"If you were figuring to hide out."

The marshal shrugged. "Most anywhere. South to Cheyenne or Laramie—"

"There are Army camps at both places."

"Well, Nebraska, Ogallala. Or down to Kansas. They do a right smart amount of card playing in Wichita and Dodge City. On the other hand, if a fella really wanted to skip, and still wanted to earn his way, there's the diggings in Montana. Deer Lodge, Virginia City. And from there it's only a running jump to Oregon. Only, a man'd be crazy to head in that direction, with the Sioux out the way they are."

Leach's forehead creased in thought. "O'Hara's not a timid man, I'll say that for him."

"A man deserts from the Army's got nerve, or he's a fool," the marshal said. "Me, I've had people lookin' for me in my time, but never the United States Government. I wouldn't like it if they was after me."

Leach said to Otto, the proprietor of the store: "Did he let drop any hint of which direction he was going to travel?"

"He didn't say he was goin' to travel."

Leach hesitated a moment, then nodding, turned toward the door. Selby was at his heels as he left the store.

Next door was a blacksmith shop and livery stable. The smith was still banging away at his anvil as Leach and the marshal entered.

"I'm looking for a deserter," Leach said to the smith, "a man with a government horse; I thought he might have come in here for a new set of shoes."

"He was," said the smith. "I saw the government brand on the horse and I wondered about it, but"—looking steadily at the marshal—"it ain't always healthy to ask a man about a horse."

"You shouldda come and told me," the marshal said chidingly.

"Maybe I should, but I didn't. He stabled the horse here two nights. Gave the name of Morrison—"

"Morrison!" exclaimed Leach.

The blacksmith shrugged. "A phoney . . ."

"No—his real name. He's been using a false one all the time he was in the Army." He frowned. "From anything he said, did you get any idea of which way he intended to travel?"

"As a matter of fact, yes. He asked about the trail to Cheyenne . . ."

"Then you can eliminate Cheyenne," Selby declared.

"Not necessarily. Morrison, or O'Hara, couldn't have had the least idea that I'd be here looking for him."

"He could have guessed that *somebody* from the Army'd be after him."

Leach shook his head. "The Army doesn't look for a man that hard. It notifies the authorities in his home town, and that's about all. Out here we may make an immediate search if we think there's a chance of getting the man in a day or two, but otherwise—"

"Yet *you're* figuring on going after him?" Selby looked at Leach sharply. "Something personal?"

Leach did not reply to that. Selby nodded his head thoughtfully. "Morrison," he said softly. "Morrison and Bligh . . ."

Like a rattlesnake striking, Leach's hand shot out and gripped the shoulder of the marshal. "Where'd you hear those names?"

Selby struck savagely at Leach's hand on his shoulder. "Don't ever grab me like that!" he snarled.

"What do you know about Morrison and Bligh?" Leach asked, his eyes blazing.

"Nothing," replied Selby. "Nothing much. Only the names registered. I've got them in the back of my mind. But it seems to me there was a third name. Morrison, Bligh and . . . and . . ."

"Woodley! Herb Woodley."

"Morrison, Bligh and Woodley. Yeah, I remember them now. Years ago. Must be eight-ten years ago. I holed up with 'em once. Down in the Indian Nations. They were on the dodge after a bank job they'd pulled somewhere . . ."

"In Missouri," Leach said.

"Could be. Anyway, the job didn't pay off. Except in getting a bunch of law after them. Somebody got hurt."

"Somebody got hurt," Leach said grimly. He made an impatient gesture. "You saw them . . ."

"Once or twice," Selby coughed. "I was kinda incognito myself, you might say. Result of a little mistake in Texas. Blew over in a little while."

"Get to the point, man!"

"What's the hurry? This was six-seven years ago."

"Nine, almost ten!"

"That long ago? Mm, wouldn't hardly think so. But I guess you're right. I had that trouble with Ben Wilson in '68 and this was before then."

"Bligh," Leach gritted, "Bligh and Morrison, tell me about them."

"What about Woodley; aren't you interested in him?"

"No, he's dead. And I know something about Morrison. Bligh, what sort of a man was he? What'd he look like?"

"Bligh," Selby repeated. "Let me see, he was the oldest one of the three. I was only a squirt then myself, and Bligh looked pretty old. Close to forty. Yeah, I 'member, he was the boss of the outfit."

"You're sure he was the leader?"

"No question about it. Morrison started to shoot off his mouth once and the old man shut him up pretty quick.

Said it was Morrison's itchy finger that'd got them into the trouble."

"So it was Morrison, after all!" exclaimed Leach.

"You seem to have a personal grudge against this Morrison."

"I have. And Bligh."

"But not Woodley?"

"I told you Woodley was dead."

"How'd he die?"

"I killed him. Oh, don't worry, it was all legal. Write to the Chicago police. But I won't promise that Morrison's death will be a legal one, when I catch up with him."

"When, or if?"

"When, because I'll get him."

Selby nodded thoughtfully. "I guess maybe you will." He frowned. "Sure you're a gen-u-wine cavalry sergeant? You been talkin' like a detective all evening."

"I'm not a detective."

"I'd hate to have you on my trail if you were. In fact, I'm gettin' to feel a little sorry for this here Morrison. Nine years ago and you're still after him. Hell, they forgot that little trouble I had down in Texas in three or four months. And they never bothered me in Wichita when I went there, only a year after the Wilson business. A memory like yours isn't a good thing. For the other guy, or you, for that matter."

Leach glowered at the marshal and walked out of the blacksmith shop. Selby watched him go and shook his head.

Seventeen

FROM the smithy, Leach crossed to a two-story log building which had a sign "Hotel" over the doorway. Leach went into the tiny lobby. A grey-whiskered man was behind a counter, scowling at an open ledger.

"Evenin', captain," he greeted Leach. "Got a nice room left."

"I'm camped outside of town," Leach said, "but I want to ask you about a man who may have stayed here a day or two ago. Morrison . . ."

The hotel man turned a page and put a stubby finger on an entry. "Here it is, Samuel Morrison, Kansas City. Checked out yesterday morning."

"Did he say where he'd be going?"

"Believe he said somethin' about going home. Home's Kansas City, it says here. Say, wait a minute, he left a letter here for a man. It was picked up only a half hour ago . . ."

"By who?"

"Emigrant. Man named Quade."

"Quade came in asking for the letter?"

"Well, not exactly. He's staying here at the hotel; him and his daughter. Got two rooms."

"But he *did* ask for the letter?"

"Yes and no. He was writing his name here on the register and I was lookin' on and mentioned I had a letter here for a man named Quade. Sam Quade. He grabbed it out of my hand."

"What room's Quade occupying?"

"Two rooms, the best in the place. Upstairs, Number One and Two . . . Hey. . . !"

But Leach was already heading for the stairs. He climbed them swiftly and, reaching a narrow hall on the second floor, struck a match and looked for the numbers on the doors.

103

One match went out and he lit another and then found Room 2. A thread of light showed under the door. Leach banged on it, with his fist.

"Who is it?" asked the voice of Molly Quade.

Leach winced. "I want to talk to Sam Quade."

"He's in Number ..." began Molly, then stopped. Leach heard a quick step inside the room, then the door was pulled open.

"You!" Molly exclaimed.

"I was looking for your father," Leach said evenly.

Her eyes went to the room next door and even as she looked the door was opened and Sam Quade stepped out into the hall.

"Here, what's this?" Quade growled. Then he recognized Leach. "What do you want with me?"

"I want to ask you some questions."

"I've got no answers for the likes of you," Quade snapped. "I thought I'd seen the last of you."

"You're going to see more of me than you like," Leach retorted. "O'Hara left a letter here for you."

"What of it?"

"I want to see that letter."

Quade snorted. "Anything else you'd like from me? My money, maybe. You've got just as good a chance of getting it."

"Quade," Leach said ominously, "I'm through bandying words with you. O'Hara's a deserter from the United States Army. By helping him escape you're an accessory and subject to arrest."

Quade's jaw became slack. "You're crazy! You can't arrest me. You're nothing but a damn sergeant ..."

"In the absence of a United States Marshal, I'm the representative of the United States Government in this vicinity. Let me assure you that I know the law—I was once an attorney. If you don't produce that letter and answer my questions, so help me, I'll place you under arrest and take you back to Fort Lincoln in irons."

"You go to hell!" Quade cried hoarsely.

"Dad!" exclaimed Molly plaintively. "Please ... he means it. For some reason he's got it in for you and he'll leave no stone unturned—"

104

"Yes," snapped Quade, grasping at the straw thrown him by his daughter. "You've had it in for me ever since you found out I was a friend of O'Hara's. You're persecuting me ..."

"You can tell that to the Federal Court," Leach said coldly. "But right now, I want that letter."

"I haven't got it."

"I don't believe you," Leach replied flatly. He made a movement toward the former sutler and Quade leaped back into the doorway of Room Number 2. Leach crowded forward, followed him into the room.

Quade, seeing that Leach was pressing for a showdown, suddenly rushed for a revolver that reposed in a holster on the bed. He got his hands on it, but Leach, springing into the room, gripped his shoulder, whirled him about and tore the gun from his fist.

Behind Leach, Molly Quade came running into the room. She sprang between the two men. "Father!" she cried. "Don't fight him—he'll kill you. . . ."

"Maybe I will at that," Leach snarled. "It depends what it says in O'Hara's letter . . ."

"Damn you!" cried Quade. "Damn you to hell. Here—read the letter."

He thrust a big hand into a pocket, brought out a crumpled envelope and thrust it into Leach's hand. Leach snatched the letter and stepped back, so that the light from the wall lamp fell on him.

He smoothed out the envelope, noted the inscription on it: *"Sam Quade, Deadwood. Hold Until Called For."*

There was a single sheet of paper in the envelope. On it was scrawled:

"Sam:—
*I'm heading for the place we talked about.
I'll wait for you there.*

Dennis O'Hara."

A wave of disappointment swept over Leach. Hope had been so strong in him a moment ago. He put down the letter.

"Where?" he demanded of Quade. "Where's this place?"

"New York," snarled Quade. "Or London, England. Take your choice."

There was a heavy step out in the hall and then a quiet voice spoke: "What's the trouble here?"

It was Selby the marshal. Quade, seeing the badge on the man's vest, turned eagerly on him: "Marshal, I demand you arrest this man. He forced his way into my room and held me up . . ."

"Mmm," said Selby, "that's a rather serious charge."

"It's a lie," Leach snapped. Then he took a quick step toward the marshal. "Selby, you said you'd met Bligh and Morrison, down in the—I mean, years ago. Look at this man. Look at him closely . . . have you ever seen him before?"

Selby looked sharply at Leach, then came forward. He surveyed Quade for a long time, then looked inquiringly at Leach.

"Who's he supposed to be?"

Leach groaned. "Look at him again, try to imagine him nine years younger . . . without a beard . . . !"

"What the devil are you driving at, Leach?" cried Quade.

Selby stared again at Quade and slowly shook his head.

"No," he said, "I've never seen him before."

"Bligh," Leach said desperately. "He's Billy Bligh . . . isn't he?"

"Maybe," said Selby, "but not the Bligh I met. I'd know *him* anywhere—nine years or no." He grinned crookedly. "I told you we holed up together for a spell."

"You're sure, man?"

"I'm sure. This isn't Billy Bligh . . . or Sam Morrison."

Leach was crushed. He dropped the letter and, stepping around Selby, headed for the door. But the marshal called to him: "Sergeant, we haven't settled this little business here."

Leach stopped in the doorway. "Forget it."

"Can't," said Selby. "Landlord downstairs complained of a racket up here and this—this man says you broke in and tried to hold him up."

106

"Yes," Quade said eagerly, "that's right. I demand you arrest him, Marshal . . ."

Then Molly Quade took a hand. "It's all a misunderstanding, Marshal. Father doesn't mean it."

Quade shot a quick glance at his daughter, then hesitated. Finally, he sighed: "All right, forget it."

"Sure," Selby said, "only I can't. I'm the marshal and—"

"You're not arresting me, Selby!" Leach snapped.

"I told you, soldier or not—"

"Don't try it, Selby," Leach said flatly. "I've got thirty-two soldiers who'll tear down your jail."

Selby's eyes glowed, but he made no move toward Leach and the latter suddenly stepped through the door and started for the stairs. He clumped heavily down to the lobby, where the hotelkeeper winced when he saw him. But Leach, without speaking to him, walked out of the hotel.

Returning to the trooper's encampment, he posted a couple of guards and rolled into his blankets.

The next day, Leach took the troop to a forest of burned-over trees, from which Deadwood had originally received its name. The men carried the saws and axes that Leach had purchased, on requisition, from the store the night before.

He put the men to felling trees and cutting them into building lengths. When some of the logs were ready, he dispatched troopers back to the camp for horses and soon they were hauling logs to the site Leach had selected for a barracks.

On the second day the men began raising the logs for a two-story building, some twenty by forty feet in size. The walls were up by the evening of the third day, when Lieutenant Brown, Second Lieutenant Brown, newly assigned to Troop M arrived in Deadwood with an escort of eight men.

He introduced himself to Leach and praised him for the work on the barracks. "You didn't lose any time, Sergeant. Good. Good. It'll make a snug place for the winter."

107

"The troop's wintering here, sir?"

"The men that are here, yes. The rest stay with the regiment at Fort Lincoln. But they'll be out this way in the spring, you can count on that."

"But what about me?"

"You stay here. Lieutenant Gregson said that since two-thirds of the troop were here, he thought it best that the First Sergeant be with them." He hesitated. "I'll be frank, Sergeant; Lieutenant Gregson told me a bit about you." He added quickly: "He thought you might, ah, act somewhat rashly and he said to tell you that he considered this post to be in the enemy's territory. In other words, this is active duty."

"I understand," Leach said. "And I'll assure you, I have no intentions of deserting." Under his breath he added: "Not now."

Which was true. O'Hara was gone. North, south, east or west. Leach didn't know. But Sam Quade knew and Sam Quade would be joining O'Hara. But not for awhile, for the day before, Quade had bought a store in Deadwood City, a general merchandise store. He intended to winter in Deadwood.

Very well, Leach would winter here, too. And in the spring, when Quade left, Leach would be following him.

Eighteen

THE winter passed in Deadwood. Not without incident, for the Black Hills, in spite of an unusually severe winter and heavy snowfall, were alive with rumors and scares. A winter military campaign was talked about in the newspapers.

Lieutenant Brown's command was alerted several times, actually received marching orders once, although they were countermanded before the troop could move out.

An expedition was being assembled to the north and west, up in Montana Territory. It was supposed to sweep eastward, down into Wyoming and Dakota. And in the east the Seventh Cavalry was being reinforced. In spring it would move west. Between it and the command in the west would be the hostiles, the Sioux and Cheyennes, who had refused to go to their reservations.

General Terry was to command the whole. Under him, in the west, was General Sully and in the east, well, who else could command the Seventh but Longhair himself? Brevet Major General George Armstrong Custer, Lieutenant-Colonel of the Seventh Cavalry, which had already made its mark in Indian fighting.

Only . . . Custer was in Washington. Somehow he had become involved in the trial of the Secretary of War. He had long been an enemy of Belknap, Grant's secretary, and he had volunteered testimony against him.

Newspapers trickled into Deadwood. Custer was in trouble. He had stepped on the toes of the President himself. He was facing a court-martial—the second in his Army career. His testimony against Belknap had fizzled; things Custer had said to the court, and to the press, for Custer could never be still in the presence of a newspaperman, had offended Grant.

The Seventh would fight that summer, but it would fight without Custer.

The balance of Troop M of the Seventh Cavalry came to Deadwood. The troop was swelled to full wartime strength and was once more commanded by Captain Holterman, at last recovered from his wounds of the fight at Nelson's Island. Lieutenant Gregson was the first lieutenant of the troop and there was another new second lieutenant, Lieutenant Lacy.

Little Fiore sported a set of corporal's chevrons and Cecil Potts, the English soldier of fortune, wore the broad yellow stripes of a sergeant.

Fiore, Potts and Leach celebrated the reunion in a saloon in Deadwood. Fiore picked a fight with a drunken mule skinner and got whipped, whereupon Potts took over Fiore's fight and beat the mule skinner. A table and a couple of chairs, not to mention some glasses, were broken in the fight.

"There go my stripes," Potts lamented.

Selby, the marshal, came into the saloon, summoned by a bartender. He surveyed the damage and cocked an eye at Leach, who was leaning against the bar.

"Your fight, Leach?" he asked.

"Count me in—they're my friends," snapped Leach.

"S'all right," Selby retorted. "I just want to see that Wolfe doesn't pad his bill for damages. About fourteen dollars, I'd say, wouldn't you?"

Leach looked at the marshal curiously. "That's all?"

"What else do you expect?"

"No arrests?"

Selby spread out his hands, palms down. "I ain't got the authority to arrest soldiers."

"You were going to take it last fall."

"I was new in the game then. Besides ..." he paused. "I'm quittin' in a couple of days."

"You're resigning your office?"

"Yep. Job's all right in winter, but it'll be summer soon and I'd like to move around again. Thought I might go back to Kansas."

Leach, half-drunk a few minutes ago, suddenly seemed oddly sober. He left the saloon with his friends and went

110

to another, where he had three more beers. They had no effect on him.

He finally said to Potts: "There's no point in me drinking. I can't feel a thing."

"Do you have to feel anything?" Potts demanded. "Can't you just drink for the fun of it?"

"I drink for the effect," Leach said. "I don't like the taste of the stuff. I'm going back to the barracks and go to bed."

Fiore and Potts protested, but Leach left them in the saloon. Outside, the sky was studded with a million stars and the narrow street that followed the canyon in which Deadwood was built was almost as bright as day.

Leach, crossing to get to the side on which the barracks was built, saw a man come out of a darkened store. It was Selby the marshal, and the store was the one that Sam Quade had bought in the fall.

"Been visiting the Quades?" Leach asked.

Selby stopped and in the moonlight, Leach could see his habitual crooked grin. "Be blind if I wouldn't. That Molly gal's all right."

"I thought gun fighting was your trade, Selby?"

"Now, Leach, you're not trying to pick a fight with me, are you?"

"I don't think there've been many friendly words between us, have there?"

"You've given me the rough edge of your tongue pretty often this past winter," Selby said evenly. "I've taken it and I'm not a man who dodges a fight. But I'll not fight a soldier."

"Patriotic?"

"Not necessarily. I just don't want any trouble."

"You didn't used to walk out of your way to avoid it."

"That was before I ..." Selby broke off. "What are you trying to do—bait me?"

"You started to say before you ... something or other? Before you fell in love?"

"Stop it, Leach."

"Or, before you struck it rich, Selby? Is Quade paying you for protection?"

"I don't know what you're talking about."

111

"I asked you once if Quade was a man you'd known before. You said he wasn't, but I've been watching you all winter, Selby. You've been in Quade's place a good many times and as a result of it, you've changed. You *dodge* fights, Selby."

"Go to hell," snapped Selby and walked off.

Leach remained standing in the middle of the street and watched Selby walk to his office and disappear inside. Then Leach walked back to the troop barracks.

Captain Holterman was seated in the small orderly room, reading some dispatches that had apparently arrived only a short time ago. He looked up as Leach entered.

"It won't be long, Sergeant," he said, shaking his head. "Nelson's Island will seem like a barroom brawl before this summer's over." He picked up an order from Fort Lincoln. "And still they want to travel through that country."

"Who, sir?"

"A party of emigrants has asked for an escort to the Montana gold fields. I've been ordered to give them a dozen men. As if twelve soldiers would be of any use. I'm tempted to refuse the escort. Just throwing away the lives of good troopers that we might need later." Captain Holterman pursed his lips. "What about Sergeant Potts?"

"He's a good man, sir."

"Wounded at Nelson's Island, wasn't he?"

"Yes, sir, but he's all right now. Only . . ."

"Yes?"

"Well, Potts in my friend, sir, and . . ."

"Every man in the troop is *my* friend," Captain Holterman said. "I've got to send somebody and Potts is a veteran. When he comes in you might tell him that he can pick his own men. They start tomorrow morning."

"From here?"

"Yes, of course."

"I didn't know a train was forming in Deadwood."

"It's a pretty small train. A dozen wagons. Evidently planned for some time, as they wrote to Fort Lincoln for the escort." The captain sighed and putting down the dispatches got to his feet. "If Sergeant Potts isn't in his

quarters, you'd better send out a man to bring him in."
He winked. "He'll need a bit of rest."

"Yes, sir."

The captain went out and Leach frowned at the door.
Potts was a good soldier, but he was reckless. The wagon
train was a small one, too. It wouldn't carry many rifles
and the way the Indians were out this summer . . .

Leach sighed and glanced at the papers on his desk. A
name leaped out from the top sheet. Sam Quade. It was
on the order for the wagon train escort: "To escort Sam
Quade and party . . ." the order read. To Virginia City,
Montana.

Leach seated himself at the desk and for long moments
stared sightlessly at the wall beyond. He had reached the
crossroads of his life. His future depended upon which
road he took. He knew well the consequences, but even as
he thought of it, he knew, too, that there was only one
choice he could make. The wrong one, yes, but for Leach,
the only one.

The years had been too long, too bitter.

He got to his feet, left the barracks, and walked back
into the town. He found Potts and Fiore still in the
saloon.

"Cecil," he said to Potts, "get back to the barracks."

"What the hell for?"

"Because you're getting up at dawn to take out a party
of emigrants."

"Who, me?"

"Captain Holterman's orders. You take twelve men for
an escort. Right through the Indian country into Montana."

Potts leered drunkenly at Leach. "You're kidding?"

"You won't think so this time tomorrow."

Potts still refused to believe, but Leach persisted and
finally, with the aid of Fiore dragged his friend out of the
saloon and back to the barracks. He saw him fall on his
cot, then went to his own quarters.

Quickly he got his few personal things together, rolled
them into a blanket and got extra ammunition for both
his carbine and six gun. Then, sighing heavily, he left the
barracks and went to the stables where the mounts of

Troop M were quartered. There was a soldier on guard there, but he did not question Leach. Instead he helped him saddle his horse.

A few minutes after midnight, Leach rode out of Deadwood.

Nineteen

DAWN found Leach huddled over a tiny fire, a dozen miles from Deadwood. From where he sat on a low promontory overlooking the northwestern trail a quarter of a mile away, he could see a couple of miles in the direction of Deadwood and to the west, a distance of four or five miles.

It was a clear, chilly morning, with considerable dew upon the grass.

A first sergeant had a certain amount of leeway and if his absence was noted at Deadwood that morning, nothing would be thought amiss. Lieutenant Gregson, who knew Leach's history, might confide in the captain, but even so, searching parties for deserters would not be sent out, with the Indians on the loose. Better lose a man than a searching party.

The sun came grudgingly over the hills in the east and Leach allowed his little fire to go out. After awhile he got to his feet and, mounting his horse, rode down to the trail. He jogged along for a couple of hours, as the sun rose in the sky, then seeing dust ahead, left the trail for the shelter of a coulee near by.

From it he watched the approach of a stagecoach, pulled by two horses, with another trailing from a lead rope. A frown creased Leach's forehead. Stages usually had six horses, never less than four. Something had happened to the coach.

On an impulse he leaped into the saddle and rode down to the trail to intercept the coach. His uniform was sufficient password to pull up the stage.

"What happened?" he called to the driver, noting a dirty, stained bandage about the man's forehead.

"Sioux," replied the driver, expectorating tobacco juice. "We pulled into the stage station last night and they was

115

there, waitin' for us. Only a small party, but they got both my passengers and the horses."

"What about the people at the station?"

"What do *you* think?"

Leach nodded. "You'll run into a wagon train with an Army escort a few miles down the road. Tell them what happened."

"I shore will." The driver cocked his head to one side. "Scoutin'?"

Leach shrugged and kneed his horse, so that it pranced away from the stagecoach. He waved to the man and started up the trail.

They would have word of his whereabouts now in Deadwood. A sergeant, alone on the westward trail. Well, it couldn't be helped.

He followed the trail until the stagecoach in his rear was out of sight, then turned off and took to the rough country. Toward noon he shot a rabbit and cooked it over a small fire. He ate all of it, then took to the saddle again. An hour later he saw a thin thread of smoke to the left and, riding in that direction, found the remains of the stage station, which the Indians had apparently fired after their ambush of the stageoach. He also found several mutilated bodies.

Leach made a wide circle about the burned stage station and picked up the trail of a number of unshod horses. It led to the west and he followed it until the trail was split into two. He made out that there were a half dozen or so horses in each group, too few to attack any but very small groups. He gave up the trail, then, and cut back to the wagon road to the south.

Where the road crossed a shallow stream Leach found the dead embers of many campfires and guessed that this was the usual campsite of emigrant trains, one day out of Deadwood. Sam Quade's little train would probably stop here for the night.

Leach searched the vicinity and found a coulee a mile to a mile and a half from the stream crossing. He hobbled his horse and, to make doubly certain that it would not stray, staked it out on a picket line. Then lying down on the grass, he watched the road below.

A half hour before sunset a rider appeared up the road. The point of the cavalry escort. Yes, a quarter mile to the rear came another rider and behind him the head of the wagon train.

Leach watched the wagons as they approached the stream. The lead one came to a halt, then the others formed a small, tight circle. The horses were staked out on picket lines, close to the wagons. Campfires went up and Leach tightened his belt a notch. The rabbit had been a small one and he had eaten nothing else all day.

Night fell over the hills and Leach could see the lights of the campfires below. He knew that Sergeant Potts would have sentries out, but his force was a small one and the sentries would have to remain pretty close to the camp.

Two hours after sundown Leach got his horse and, mounting, made a great circle about the camp at a distance of at least a mile. As far as he could tell there were no hostiles in the vicinity. He staked the horse again in the coulee then, and rolled himself up in his blanket.

At dawn he was up and in the saddle. Circling the camp, where breakfast fires had been started, he rode ahead on the wagon road, a half dozen miles, then tying his horse to a small tree, he sat down on the ground a few yards from the road.

An hour went by and a rider appeared on the road. He was a mile distant. Leach got to his feet and went to his horse. He mounted and started down the road to meet the rider. Before he had gone halfway, the report of a rifle rolled to Leach. The point had signaled the train.

Leach put his horse into a trot. Ahead, the trooper turned his horse sidewards, ready for a swift retreat if it was necessary, but suddenly the rider again turned his horse toward Leach and actually came forward.

Then Leach recognized the man. It was Corporal Fiore.

"Leach!" the little man cried when still some distance away. "What the devil are you doing out here?"

Leach began pulling up his horse. "Fiore," he said. "It's good to see you."

117

"Huh!" exclaimed Fiore, trying to control his prancing horse. "You saw me only night before last."

"Then you don't know?"

"Know what?"

"That I've deserted?"

The little corporal's jaw became slack. "What'd you say?"

"I've deserted."

"You're crazy!"

Leach shook his head. "I left Deadwood yesterday morning, before you did."

Fiore stared at Leach, then turned his horse as another mount came pounding up; it was ridden by another trooper.

"Sergeant!" exclaimed the second trooper. "Didn't expect to see you out here."

The head of the wagon train appeared around a low knoll, a quarter of a mile away. Leach said to the troopers: "I want to have a talk with Potts."

He kneed his horse and the animal sprang ahead. It broke into a swift gallop that quickly ate up the distance to the wagon train. As he approached, Leach knew that he was recognized for Potts came forward to meet him.

"So you're the sergeant the stage driver told us about yesterday," Potts cried.

"I am, Cecil." Leach drew a deep breath. "You don't know that I've deserted?"

Potts hesitated. "I know you weren't at the barracks yesterday morning when we pulled out. Lieutenant Gregson and Captain Holterman seemed pretty excited about something and I heard them mention your name. Then yesterday, when that stage driver described a soldier with a top sergeant's chevrons, well, I got to wondering . . ."

Leach, looking past Potts, saw a man riding forward from the wagon train. He said quickly to Potts: "Ride ahead with me."

"Sure," said Sergeant Potts, spurring his horse.

The two men distanced the rider from the wagon train, then pulled up their horses. Potts said, then: "This part of your old trouble?"

118

Leach countered: "Quade's running this wagon train, isn't he?"

"That's right, but I don't see—"

"He's going to meet O'Hara, somewhere in Montana."

Potts blinked. "You mean O'Hara's behind all this?"

"He's one of the two men I've been looking for, all these years," Leach said grimly. "And I think Sam Quade's the other."

Potts whistled softly. "O'Hara, I'm willing to believe. But Quade, man, he's got a daughter . . . and she's here with him."

"The fool!" Leach said, bitterly. "Taking a woman on a trip like this."

"Hell, we got six women with us. And three-four kids."

"You saw what happened at that stage station yesterday?"

"Of course." Potts shrugged. "I'm a soldier; you are yourself, Leach. We take orders . . ."

"Not I—not any more. I'm through with the Army."

Potts' forehead creased. "I haven't any official word, but . . . you're admitting you're a deserter?"

"To you, yes." Then Leach grimaced and looked ahead. "And I told Joe Fiore."

"Damn," said Potts. "You put me in an awful spot . . ."

Behind them came the galloping of horses' hoofs. Leach, shooting a glance over his shoulder, saw that the man from the wagon train was making a determined effort to catch up with them. He relaxed his grip on the reins, then suddenly tightened them.

"That's Dick Selby, the marshal!"

"Yeah," said Potts. "He's with the wagon train."

"He's going to Montana with you? Then I'm *right* . . . ! I guessed it in Deadwood and this is the confirmation."

Selby pounded up. "Leach!" he exclaimed. "I thought I recognized you. What kind of a damn trick do you call this? Send your soldiers out with one man in command, then chase after and take over from him."

"So you're following Quade to Montana," Leach said coldly. "I called the turn; you've thrown in with O'Hara." His lips curled contemptuously. "What's he paying you?"

119

"Not a damn cent, Leach. I'm going to Montana for my own reasons. This wagon train just happened to be leaving and I thought I'd go along."

"Stick to that story," Leach said through bared teeth. "Stick to it to the end."

Selby wheeled his horse and went back to the wagon train. Potts watched him soberly. "That man's a notorious gun fighter, Leach. Did you know?"

"He could be Wild Bill Hickok, for all I care."

Potts inhaled deeply. "What about you?"

"I'd like to travel with you, Cecil." Then, as Potts hesitated: "You can't deliver me back to Deadwood because you can't spare the men. Besides, you weren't told officially that I was a deserter."

Potts squinted. "That's spitting in the soup, lad. I've done a lot of soldiering in my time. In two or three different armies. Ignorance is no excuse; I've found that out." Then suddenly he grunted. "But what the hell could they do—break me? I've had stripes a dozen times. Sure, lad, ride along with us. You've got sense enough to escape from my clumsy hands when the time is right." He looked morosely off to the undulating hills. "Although, I'm thinkin' a lot's going to happen before any of us sees an Army fort again."

"You're right, Cecil. All of our scalps may be decorating the lodges of the Sioux."

Potts swore bitterly. "And these blasted emigrants have got to go looking for trouble! What difference does it make to them whether they're in Alder Gulch or Deadwood? There's gold in both places; you still have to dig for it, no matter where you are."

Twenty

TOWARD sundown, when the wagon train was looking for a suitable camping ground, a man came along the trail, from the direction of Deadwood. He came at a good clip and his horse looked to be in pretty bad shape. He stopped and dismounted to give the animal a breather.

"Custer's back," he announced to the soldiers. "He's been reinstated and he's going to lead the regiment from Bismarck in a day or two."

A cheer went up among the soldiers. "The Sioux better get back to their reservations," one man declared.

The man, who wore a buckskin suit of clothes, spat on the ground. "They won't get off that easy," he said. "Longhair'll teach Sitting Bull and Rain-in-the-Face the same kind of lesson he taught Black Kettle down on the Washita. They'll fight because he'll *make* them fight . . . I'm taking dispatches to General Sully." Crouched on the ground, he looked up at Leach. "A first sergeant's been posted at Deadwood as a deserter," he said casually.

"So I've heard," Leach replied grimly.

"Yeah? He wasn't spotted until last night."

"I'm the deserter."

The dispatch bearer chuckled. "Thought you might be."

"Anything you figure to do about it?"

"Me? I'm carrying dispatches. That's enough of a job for one man."

"You'll be riding back this way?"

The man shook his head. "I'm riskin' my hair once. By the law of averages I might get away with it, but I ain't going to crowd my luck. When I get to the General I keep goin'—in the other direction." He got to his feet. "Well, I guess I'll make a few more miles."

He ran to his horse and vaulted into the saddle. In a

moment he was off, waving to the soldiers and the wagon train.

The news that Custer was back with the Seventh and would be in the field in a few days cheered the members of the wagon train as well the soldiers.

Custer would be moving straight west from Bismarck, into the heart of the Sioux Country. His approach would be the rallying signal for the Indians. They would head north from Wyoming and travel at top speed. The wagon train would stand a good chance of getting through, for it was skirting the southern part of the Indian country.

Night fell swiftly in the foothills and those of the soldiers not assigned to guard duty rolled themselves into their blankets.

Potts consulted Leach about the posting of the guards. "You went through this last fall, Leach. What do you think—are the sentries out far enough?"

"No," replied Leach, "but you haven't got the men to put them out further. However, I've never heard of Indians attacking at night. They may try to stampede the horses, but I doubt if they'll make an all-out fight in the dark."

"Then why don't we put the horses inside the wagon circle?"

"Too many animals for the small amount of grass, Cecil. You've got to travel fast and far every day and the horses can't do it without plenty of forage."

A man came up from the wagon train. It was Sam Quade. He had already learned from Selby of Leach's presence and scowled at him.

"You in command of these soldiers, Leach?"

"No, Sergeant Potts is."

Quade grunted. "The people in the train heard you were here and knowing that you pulled through the train last fall, they want you to take command . . ."

"Can't," Leach replied laconically. "I'm going along, but Sergeant Potts is in command."

"Why, if you're a top sergeant and he's just a plain sergeant?"

"It's a long story, Quade. I'm not going into it. Maybe if you think about it, you'll guess the answer yourself."

122

"It's because of me, eh? All right, we'll settle our differences when we're through this . . ."

Leach sprang to his feet. "You're admitting you're Billy Bligh?"

"Don't be a fool; I'm not admitting anything, except that my name is Sam Quade. But we've got a bunch of people in this train and we're in Indian country. We want to get through—safely, so . . ." He cleared his throat. "So I'm offering the services of our men for sentry duty and such."

"We could use them," Potts declared promptly.

Quade nodded. "Leach had trouble getting the emigrants to help the last time, but I'm not fool enough for that. You tell me how many men you want and where you want them."

Potts shot a look at Leach. "The horses," the latter said. "Leaves your men free to make the rounds."

Potts accepted the services of a half dozen emigrants and posted them over the horses of both the wagon train and the cavalrymen.

The night passed without incident and the next day the wagon train reeled off another twenty miles over easy, rolling terrain. This was the third day out from Deadwood and the train was well into the northeast corner of Wyoming, heading for the Montana line, another three or four days distant. There the train would take a more westerly course, traveling most of the great expanse of Montana Territory, two weeks of good traveling.

Of Indians the wagon train saw nothing, but there were smoke signals in the sky the following day and the train crossed the trail of a large band, heading north. Leach rode away from the emigrant train, following the trail for a couple of miles until he came to a creek, where the unshod hoofs of the horses were plain in the sandy banks. He guessed then that there were easily a hundred horses in the war party. He rode swiftly back to the train and found it halted.

"What's up?" Leach asked of a group of emigrants who were looking off to the west.

"One of the soldiers made a signal," was the reply. "The sergeant rode up to see what's up."

Leach saw Potts come galloping back and rode out to meet him.

"There's an Indian village over that ridge," Potts said, when he reached Leach. "Forty or fifty lodges, but only a half dozen horses around it."

"Must be the women and children then," Leach said. "I guess that's where the war party came from."

"What do we do? Go around?"

Leach studied the terrain ahead. The ridge was a long low one, rising to the south and eventually becoming a mountain. It fell away to the right, but in that direction the war party had gone.

"If you try to skirt that mountain you lose at least a day; maybe more. And I don't think you want to circle to the north. I don't see that it makes much difference. If the village is just over the ridge, they know about you by now anyway. There are always some old men and boys left in the villages."

"You think we should go straight through?"

"It's a tough decision to make, but how do you know? There might be a bigger village in the mountains to the south—with warriors in it. I'm convinced that this territory is swarming with Indians."

"Damnit, I wish I was back in Fort Lincoln," exclaimed Potts. "Or at least Deadwood."

They rode back to the emigrant train and Potts explained the situation to Quade and the other men of the group.

"I say, go straight ahead and burn the damn village," Selby, the ex-marshal, declared. "That's what Custer did on the Washita. Wipe out every damn man, woman and child."

"You do that and you're inviting the massacre of this train!" Leach said quickly.

"They'd massacre us anyway if they were strong enough," Selby retorted.

His plan, however, found no favor with the emigrants and after a little discussion it was decided to go straight through the valley, without molesting the village.

The wagons started off and the troopers rode alongside of it, on the southerly side, strung out in a thin line;

124

twelve soldiers, counting Leach and not counting the two men who ride in advance.

Slowly the train crested the low ridge and started down into the broad valley beyond. The Indian village was sprawled along the north bank of a small stream. Smoke issued from some of the lodges, but no Indians could be seen.

The wagons rolled down the incline, keeping close together. They would pass the village at a distance of about a hundred yards. Leach and Potts, riding at the head, watched the tents closely. There was movement in them, but whoever was inside feared to come out into the open.

The wagon train came abreast of the tents; in length it was just about as long as the forty or fifty lodges. Leach and Potts passed the last tent, then Leach turned his horse.

A hundred feet back, an Indian boy of twelve or thirteen suddenly darted out of a tent. There was a bow in his hands and an arrow strung in it.

He let fly with the arrow, at one of the wagons. The shaft fell far short, sticking upright into the ground.

A horse broke out from the emigrant line; it headed straight for the Indian boy, who was fitting a second arrow to his bow. Leach cried out hoarsely and drove spurs into his horse's flanks.

But he was too late. A revolver in the hand of the other horseman barked and the Indian lad was hurled violently to the ground.

An Indian squaw darted out of the nearest tent, screaming. She threw herself upon the boy. The killer of the young Indian pulled his horse back to its haunches, let fly a second shot, this time at the squaw. She was hit, but apparently not seriously, for she bounced to her feet, yelling at the top of her lungs.

She started running down the line of tents. The man on horseback, Dick Selby, sent another bullet after her, missing.

Leach, by this time, was bearing down on Selby. His eyes blazing in fury, he whipped out his Colt and galloping alongside of Selby, struck out with the barrel of the

125

weapon. It caught the ex-marshal at the base of his skull and dropped him out of the saddle.

Selby hit the ground heavily, half scrambled to his knees, then collapsed, groaning. Leach whirled his horse, rode back and looked down at the moaning man.

"Damn you, Selby," he cried. "I warned you." He raised his gun again, but at that moment a couple of emigrants dashed up on their horses. And Sergeant Potts came between Leach and Selby.

"Don't, lad!" he cried. "It was a foul thing he did, but you've done enough."

"He murdered that boy in cold blood," Leach raged. "He couldn't have hurt anyone with that small bow. And Selby shot the squaw because she came out to throw herself upon her murdered child. The man's kill-crazy and better off dead . . ."

A gun banged. Leach, whirling, shot a quick glance down the line of tents. An aged Indian was standing in front of the last tent, an ancient musket in his hands.

"Let's get out of here before somebody gets hurt," Sergeant Potts cried. "We don't want to hurt any more of these people, but they'll bring the whole tribe down on us."

A couple of the emigrants were already helping Selby to his feet. The man couldn't walk by himself, but they started propelling him toward the wagons.

Indian women, as well as boys and a few old men, were now pouring out of the tents. A few arrows were shot at the emigrants and a couple of guns went off, but nobody was hurt.

Leach signaled to Potts. "Get them moving—fast!"

Somewhere behind the tents, a puff of smoke shot up into the sky, then another and still another.

"Signals!" groaned Potts. He roared to the emigrants. "Get moving—on the double!"

He and Leach pelted back to the head of the column. The wagons started rolling and then every Indian from the village swarmed out. Women screamed imprecations at the emigrants and soldiers, threw stones and sticks. A shower of arrows went out at the rear wagons, some of

126

them sticking in the canvas, a few prodding horses, but doing no special damage.

On a dead run the wagons tore off. Leach, looking over his shoulder, saw the smoke signals going up into the sky and shook his head.

"Better start looking for a place to make a stand," he shouted to Sergeant Potts.

The wagons were going downhill and making good speed, but the horses could not keep up the breakneck pace for long and inside of a mile the train was strung out along the valley, with ragged intervals between the wagons.

Leach galloped back along the line and told the drivers to slacken their pace and keep closed up, but it was useless. The emigrants were frightened and each driver was determined to go his own best speed.

A half dozen Indian boys, who had somehow found scrawny ponies, were harrying the rear of the train. One or two had guns and were banging away. Leach ordered a couple of soldiers to ride back and drive them off.

The men charged the young Indians and dispersed them, but when they rejoined the train, the Indians were back again, at the rear.

Then it happened. A wagon, near the head of the column, hit a prairie dog hole, bounced into the air and coming down, snapped an axle. The driver of the wagon jumped to the ground and tried to stop another wagon, but the second wagon swerved around him and continued at breakneck speed. There were a woman and two children in the back of the disabled wagon.

Leach drew his revolver and galloped his horse to the head of the train. Wheeling, he fired a couple of shots into the air and forced his mount into the path of the first wagon. He had to swerve his horse aside, but the wagon pulled up.

"Keep out of my way, soldier!" the driver cried.

"This is as far as you go," Leach yelled back. "The train travels together, or it doesn't move . . ."

"Oh, yeah?" retorted the driver. He caught up a rifle that lay on the seat beside him. And then he dropped it again as Leach sent a bullet into the canvas cover of the wagon, inches from the driver's head.

Sergeant Potts pounded up.

"Spread your men out here, Potts. Don't let a wagon pass," Leach ordered.

Without questioning Leach's decision, Potts signaled to his men and quickly deployed them so that each wagon had to stop as it came up.

"There's a wagon with a broken axle," Leach announced, then to the emigrants: "When it's ready to move again, the train moves. Not before."

"You want us to get massacred?" cried an emigrant.

"Do you expect to outrun Indians on ponies with these wagons?" Leach snapped. "What's the difference whether you fight here, or . . . ?" He started to say, "five miles from here," but found it was unnecessary. The two soldiers from the point were galloping back, both firing their rifles.

"Make your circle!" Leach roared. "Your fight's come to you."

One moment the prairie had seemed deserted, then suddenly it was filled with Indians, coming from the west and north, in a broad semicircle.

"Never mind the circle!" Leach cried. "You haven't got time. Down . . . fight for your lives."

The soldiers were already springing from their saddles. The bleating of the women in the emigrant train, the hoarse cries of the men, and the screeching of the approaching Indians drowned out Leach's commands and the soldiers dropped wherever they leaped from their horses. The guns of the emigrants began banging away and the soldiers opened fire, before the Indians were really within good range.

There was no orderly fire, no discipline among the defenders. Not that it would have made any difference in the eventual result, for there were fully two hundred Indians in the attacking war party, as against not more than twenty-five rifles among the emigrants and soldiers.

Indians plummeted from the saddles as individual marksmen picked them off. But it was as isolated drops of rain beating against a windowpane.

The Indians came on, a hundred yards, fifty. A woman in the emigrant party screamed and, suddenly springing to her feet, started running. A man leaped up to bring her back, was riddled with bullets. Men rose to their knees, their feet, as the wave of Indians bore down. Others died on the ground.

The Indian horde hit the emigrants and without even faltering swarmed through and over them. Horses trampled men, women and children. Tomahawks flashed and thudded into skulls and bodies. Lances pierced a man here and there.

The force of the attack carried the Indians beyond the emigrants, but, whirling, they came back. Leach, who had emptied his six shooter into the Indians, now caught up a carbine. He pulled the trigger in the face of a savagely painted redskin charging down on him. The gun failed to fire, either because the cartridge was defective or because the gun was empty.

He started to throw up the barrel of the gun to take the blow of a tomahawk in the Indian's hand and then—then lightning struck him from the rear. Leach went down and out.

Twenty-one

EXCRUCIATING pain lanced from Leach's head down into his body. A tomahawk seemed to be smashing him intermittently upon the head and Leach put up his hands to ward off the blows. To no avail.

Leach forced open his eyes and with a rush recovered full consciousness and found that he was lying in the bed of a wagon and the crashing blows were the result of his head bouncing on the floorboards, with every jolt of the wagon.

He sat up—and looked into the painted face of an Indian, crouched on his haunches just inside the tailgate of the wagon. A tomahawk was in his greasy fist and he raised it as Leach sat up.

Leach groaned, swiveled his aching head and saw that an Indian was driving the horses that pulled the wagon. His eyes went back to the Indian in the rear of the wagon. The man got unsteadily to his feet, made a threatening gesture with the tomahawk and Leach fell back.

For a moment he expected that his head would be split by the tomahawk and steeled himself for the blow, but when it did not come he opened his eyes and saw that the Indian had resumed his crouch.

The wagon bounced and jolted over the prairie land. By straining his ears, Leach became aware that there were other wagons to the rear and many, many horses alternately clop-clopping and galloping.

Cautiously he raised his torso once more and, a threat failing to materialize, moved a few inches and rested his back and head against a couple of sacks of meal. In that position he could look out through the rear of the wagon and see a half dozen wagons jolting along behind the one in which he was riding. And he saw Indians riding in and out of the line of wagons. One or two were wearing unbuttoned troopers' blouses.

130

A half hour went by when suddenly there was much shouting on the part of the Indians. Most of them galloped past the wagon in which Leach was traveling and in another minute or two, dogs began to bark; many dogs.

Leach, turning, saw Indian lodges, as far as his eye could see.

Leach's wagon stopped and the Indian by the tailgate got to his feet. He uttered several explosive words and hopped nimbly out of the wagon. His gesture with the tomahawk told Leach that he was to follow.

The wahooing of Indians rose to a crescendo as Leach climbed out of the wagon. Standing on the ground, he looked around at a circle of hostile faces, mostly squaws, who were being held back by threats and gestures on the part of the warriors who had brought in the captured wagon trains.

A white man fell out of the wagon behind Leach, limped to his feet. It was Sam Quade, his clothing torn, his face smeared with dried blood. After him came Molly Quade and Leach involuntarily emitted a sigh of relief.

Corporal Joe Fiore was herded forward by a couple of Indians and behind him another trooper, a huge private named Fedderson. For a moment Leach thought that these were the only survivors from the wagon train, but then two more men appeared, Dick Selby and Sergeant Cecil Potts.

An Indian with a single eagle's feather in his braided hair, stepped up to Leach and tapped him on the chest. "Come!" he said.

The Indian strode ahead of Leach. He carried a repeating Spencer carbine and with it gestured aside the squaws who crowded forward. They opened up a narrow lane and the Indian went through. Leach, following, was spat upon by the squaws and now and then struck a vicious blow with a club. He looked neither to the right or left, however, and followed the Indian to a large tent. There the warrior stopped and pointing to the door, said:
"In!"

Stooping, Leach entered the buffalo skin tent. A moment later, Quade and Molly came in; blood streamed

131

from a fresh cut on Molly's face and she was crying softly.

Quade threw himself upon the ground, but Molly stood, her hands covering her face. Fiore entered the tent, swearing softly, but stopped when he saw the girl.

Potts came in on the heels of Fiore and then, last, came Dick Selby who was literally catapulted into the crowded tent by the feet of a couple of Indians.

Potts whirled upon Selby and gave him a kick on his own account. "You're the cause of this all, damn your killing soul!"

Selby rolled over and came up to his hands and knees. "Nobody never kicked me before," he said, his face pale and twitching. "I ever get a gun in my hands again, you'll get down on your belly and beg."

"You ever see a gun again, it'll be a miracle," Potts exclaimed. Then he saw Leach.

"So *you* made it, too."

Leach nodded. "Is this all?"

"I guess so; I haven't seen or heard of anyone else." He shook his head. "I wonder why they saved us."

"Hostages," offered Corporal Fiore. But the hope died quickly in his eyes. "No, that sounds silly . . ."

Potts' mouth was a thin, straight line. "You ask me, they brought us in to have some sport." He swallowed hard. "I've heard of the Indians doing . . ." Then he caught Leach's eye and broke off.

For a moment there was an awkward silence in the tent, broken only by Molly Quade's sobbing. Sam Quade spoke then: "Never heard of Indians *capturing* wagons. Usually they burn everything."

"This is a big camp," Leach said, "and there's a lot of food in the wagons. I guess they needed it."

"Indians don't go for flour and bacon, as a rule," said Quade. "They prefer buffalo meat."

"They haven't got time to hunt," snapped Dick Selby, getting to his feet. "They're getting ready for a big fight."

"Custer!" cried Potts. "They know he's in the field." He exhaled heavily. "Did you get a look at all the lodges, Leach? How many would you say there were here?"

"Five hundred and it could be as many as a thousand."

"A thousand lodges! There aren't that many Indians in Dakota."

"We're not in Dakota now; we're in Wyoming, or maybe Montana. It isn't the Sioux alone who're out. The Cheyennes are with them, maybe some Nez Percés. This is a big village, but it isn't the only one. An all-out fight is coming."

"Custer'll take care of 'em," Corporal Fiore declared confidently. "A thousand Indians—five thousand, it won't make no difference to the Seventh. Custer's never been licked."

"Custer can't fight five thousand Indians," Leach said soberly.

"He doesn't have to. Terry's coming from the west; Terry, Gibbon and Crook. With Custer hittin' 'em from the east there won't be a Sioux left to send back to the reservations."

Molly Quade suddenly uncovered a tear-stained face and looked at Leach. "We won't be alive to know the final result; that's true, isn't it?"

Steadily Leach returned her appealing look. "We're in a tight spot."

Her mouth twisted bitterly. "So it ends here, in a miserable Indian village. How do they kill you? Do they burn you at the stake, or do they cut off your fingers, then your arms and—"

"Stop it," Leach said savagely.

She looked at him scornfully. "You didn't count on this, did you? You thought you'd go on living and hating—and seeking vengeance. You didn't think you'd meet your end here with me—with us? You're hard, John Leach, hard and cruel, but the Sioux are cruel, too. They'll do things to us that you never—"

Leach's hands shot out, gripped her arms, and shook her violently. "Stop it, I said. This is no time to get hysterical. The least we can do is show these Indians we're not afraid of them. If we've got to die—"

"—We'll die smiling!" sneered Dick Selby.

Leach struck him in the face with his open palm, a stinging blow. He hit him a second time, rocking the gun

133

fighter's head. "That's the last I'll take from you, Selby . . ."

Potts sprang forward, his hand clenched into a huge fist. "I'm with Leach, Selby. One more peep out of you and I'll cold-cock you."

Selby stepped back. The tent scraped his head and he ducked, as if somebody had struck him from behind. "You're so goddamn brave," he snarled. "You make me . . ." He broke off, as Potts stepped toward him threateningly.

An Indian with a full headdress of feathers appeared suddenly in the open doorway of the tent. His eyes searched the group and came to rest upon Leach.

"You, Sergeant," he said. "Come!"

Leach drew a deep breath and took a step toward the door. Then Molly Quade sprang forward. "John—wait!"

Leach stopped. "This isn't the time, Molly," he said quietly.

The Indian gestured violently. "Come!"

Leach stepped through the doorway. Outside the tent the Indian strode to a huge bonfire that had been built in an open space between the two rows of skin tents. The way was lined with squaws and Indian youths, who threw sticks at Leach and yelled imprecations at him.

Near the fire were gathered a dozen Indians, all wearing feather headdresses. The man who had brought Leach to the group folded his arms and fixed Leach with a cold glare.

"Where Longhair?" he suddenly barked.

"I haven't seen General Custer in months," Leach replied.

"You Seventh Cavalry. Longhair, your general."

"Yes, but I've been at Deadwood."

"Longhair come," the Indian persisted. "How many soldiers he bring?"

Leach shook his head. Like a rattlesnake striking, the Indian's arms unfolded and the back of his hand struck Leach in the mouth.

"You talk!"

"I told you," Leach said, as blood trickled from his lips down his chin, "I come from Deadwood—not Fort Lin-

134

coln. I don't know a thing about Custer, or his plans. I'm only a sergeant, not an officer."

The Indian's obsidian eyes glittered. He suddenly pointed at one of the other Indians and said something in the Siouan tongue. The Indian bobbed his head and, whirling, trotted to a tent. The first Indian refolded his arms.

The Indian came out of the tent, carrying a buckskin shirt and a large Manila envelope. He trotted back to the group and handed the articles to the Indian who was questioning Leach. The latter threw the buckskin shirt at Leach's feet.

"You know that?"

There was blood on the shirt, indication enough as to what had happened to the former wearer. But a buckskin shirt meant nothing to Leach. He shook his head.

"Him, what you call—messenger. Carry order from Longhair to General." He suddenly thrust the Manila envelope at Leach. "I read him. Say Longhair come from Dakota, meet Terry, Crook. Kill Sioux and Cheyenne."

Leach guessed then that these were the orders the courier had been carrying along the Deadwood trail, the man who had been going to Terry.

"Where Longhair?" the Indian demanded.

"I don't know."

The Indian pointed again at the man who had brought the buckskin shirt and captured orders. He spat out a couple of words and the man trotted off. This time he went into another tent. He was inside for a moment or two, then popped out and stood by the doorway.

A man came out; a man wearing a ragged Prince Albert, blood-stained shirt and torn broadcloth trousers. Dennis O'Hara, late sergeant of Troop M, of the Seventh Cavalry.

Leach stiffened. As yet O'Hara had not recognized him. He came slowly forward, his step quickening as he came nearer, even becoming a swagger.

Then he saw Leach and his step faltered. But only for a moment. He came up to the group, his lips bared in a cruel grin.

"Well, well, pardner!" he said sardonically.

135

The Indian spokesman looked at Leach and pointed at O'Hara. "Him come from west. Say general marching with five thousand soldier."

"He's a liar," Leach said, "a liar and a deserter."

"What you mean, deserter?" demanded the Indian. "Him no soldier."

"He was a sergeant in the Seventh Cavalry," Leach retorted. "He ran away—deserted. He'd tell you anything."

"Nice going, Leach," snapped O'Hara. "Maybe I can fix things for you, too." He addressed the Indian. "Him General Custer man. He know where Custer."

The Sioux's eyes glittered as they shot from Leach to O'Hara, then back to Leach.

"Last time ask. Where Custer?"

Leach made no reply. The Indian stooped suddenly, tore a tomahawk from a seated Indian's hand and leaped at Leach. The latter tried to block the blow with his arm, but the dull side of the tomahawk smashed through his guard and struck him on the side of the head. Leach went down, gasping in horrible pain. He retained consciousness, but for a moment or two was oblivious to what was going on around him. Then strong hands grabbed him under the armpits, raised him to his feet and hurled him forward. Leach fell on his face, tried to climb to his feet and a foot kicked him down again.

"Get up, Leach!" snarled a voice in his ear and hands again raised him to his feet.

Leach summoned the last of his strength and stumbled away. A hand shoved him along. Blows struck him, but Leach scarcely felt them.

And then suddenly his eyes focused for one second upon the open doorway of a tent and he fell forward. Hands dragged him into the tent.

Twenty-two

SOMEBODY dabbed at his bleeding head, but it was moments before Leach realized that he was back in the tent with the other prisoners. When his eyes finally cleared he looked up into the face of Molly Quade.

"John," Molly said softly, "are you all right?"

It was an inane question to ask, but the emotion behind the words oddly stilled the shrieking pain in his head. He smiled wanly.

Then the voice of Dennis O'Hara brought Leach up to a sitting position. O'Hara was in the tent, crouched on the far side, talking earnestly to Sam Quade.

"... They're having a big powwow tonight," O'Hara was saying. "I've learned a few words of their lingo and I made out that some high mucky-mucks in the tribes are expected. Sitting Bull, maybe. Or Rain-in-the-Face."

Leach said: "What did you tell them about the Army, O'Hara?"

O'Hara turned, looked impassively at Leach. "So you're awake again? You just had a very narrow escape."

"I said, what did you tell them, O'Hara?"

"Not a damn thing. They know Terry's coming down from the Yellowstone. They kept asking me how many men he had and I told them plenty, five thousand."

"How many has he got?"

"How should I know? Enough to wipe out this crowd, I guess."

"You didn't come from Terry's column?"

"Of course not. I wintered at Deer Lodge. I was going ..." he shrugged. "I was headed east."

"To meet Quade?"

O'Hara's lips parted in a wolfish grin. "Still harping on that!"

Leach's eyes found Selby, glowering, a few feet from

137

O'Hara and Quade. "Look at them, Selby. Do you recognize them now—Billy Bligh and Sam Morrison?"

Selby made no reply, but his eyes remained on Leach.

Leach said: "You were going to make your fortune from them, Selby. You were going with Quade to meet O'Hara. But Quade got word to O'Hara. So he was coming to meet you ... when you weren't expecting him. A little ambush ..."

"That isn't so!" cried Sam Quade.

"But it is, Selby," Leach persisted. "You know it is. You were going to be dry-gulched. Doublecrossed ..."

Molly Quade reached out and caught Leach's hand. "John, it's my turn to tell you to stop it. It's too late for all that."

"I've got to know," Leach said stubbornly.

O'Hara sprang to his feet. "Goddamn you, Leach, then know it. I'm Morrison, the man you've hounded for nine years. And he's—" stabbing his forefinger at Quade—"and he's Billy Bligh. Now, you know it and what good will it do you? You'll be dead before morning and so will all of us."

"You killed Helen Alderton," Leach said, tonelessly. "You crippled her and she lived seven months ... and died a little each day. I—I hope you don't die fast."

"I didn't even know who Helen Alderton was," snarled O'Hara. "I had nothing against her. She got in the way of a bullet, that's all. It was an accident. But you—damn you, Leach, what kind of a man are you?—following us all these years! I'm not afraid of any man alive, but damn this ghost stuff, chasing us, year after year."

"Woodley said that to me," Leach said, "as he was dying ..."

"You killed him."

"As I would have killed you, O'Hara ... or Morrison."

Outside the tent a wild hullaballoo arose among the Indians. War whoops resounded through the camp, women shrilled and guns were fired. Moccasined feet pounded past the tent. For several moments the din was so great that it was useless even to attempt conversation inside the tent of the prisoners. Then the noise subsided somewhat and O'Hara scurried to the door of the tent.

"A war party's come in, but a pretty small one. Wait ..." He cocked his head to one side, strained to listen. "They brought news. Longhair's near."

"Near here?" Leach cried.

O'Hara shook his head. "No, thirty miles to the north. He's got the entire Seventh with him—the whole Army, they say ..."

"A thousand men!" exclaimed Sam Quade.

"Not nearly," Leach said, shaking his head. "One or two hundred must have stayed behind at Fort Lincoln. And he must have another hundred or two with his baggage train and reserves. I doubt if he could muster more than seven hundred men for a fight."

"There are at least three thousand Sioux right here," O'Hara declared. "And there's a camp up at the Little Big Horn with no less than four thousand lodges."

"How do you know?"

"I almost ran into it two days ago. Then I cut down this way and ... well, they got me, anyway ..."

"Four thousand lodges," Sergeant Potts said in a tone of awe. "Ten or twelve thousand warriors ... and three thousand here. If they get the General between them ..."

"They won't," O'Hara said confidently. "He's too smart for that."

"Maybe," said Potts, "and maybe not. I'm sure he hasn't the slightest idea of how many Indians are out. The talk in Deadwood was a couple or three thousand Indians—scattered war parties of a few hundred each. They'd have called you crazy if you'd told them that ten or fifteen thousand Indians would be on the war path—in two large parties."

"Custer's foolhardy," Leach offered. "At Gettysburg he charged Stuart's entire army with a single brigade. We got cut to pieces ..."

"We?" exclaimed Potts.

O'Hara grinned wickedly. "Sure, he was there. He was with the Boy General all through the damn war. Captain John Leach of the Thirty-Second Missouri. The hero of Chancellorsville, Yellow Tavern, Custer's favorite! Why do you think he was promoted over me at Fort Lincoln?"

139

Leach ignored the jibe. He addressed Potts: "Custer ought to know what's he's going against."

Potts groaned. "There's no chance."

"We've got to try."

"There's no hope of escaping, Leach," protested Sergeant Potts. "And even if somebody *could* get away, it's thirty miles to Custer—if he stayed still. Which he won't. He'll be moving . . ."

"West." Leach looked steadily at O'Hara. "Where's the village on the Little Big Horn?"

O'Hara licked his lips with his tongue. "You're asking something of *me*, Leach?"

"You're a white man, O'Hara. And you served in the Seventh Cavalry . . . how long was it? Six years? Seven . . . ?"

O'Hara sank down to his haunches, staring at Leach. He said slowly: "Not that it'll do any good, but the Little Big Horn's twenty-five, thirty miles from here. North, northwest . . ."

With his finger, Leach drew a line on the earthen floor of the tent. "We're here," he said, pointing to the bottom of the line, "and the other Indian village is up here . . ." touching the top of the line. He drew a straight line from the top of the parallel one to a point several inches to the right. "Custer's about here . . ."

"The thing to do is to cut straight down the middle," interposed Potts. "If you travel through the night you can meet Custer before he gets to this Little Big Horn . . ."

O'Hara jeered. "And all you got to do is get away from here. Try it!"

At that point, the Indians outside again created a clamor, drowning out the voices inside the tent. O'Hara, watching the proceedings, suddenly scuttled back into the tent. A moment later the Indian who had struck Leach with the tomahawk filled the doorway.

His eyes sought Leach, found him lying on his back. "You lie," he spat. "Longhair come. Tomorrow every soldier die." He stabbed out with his forefinger. "You die tonight. And you," pointing at O'Hara. He finished with a sweeping gesture that included everyone in the tent. "All die tonight. Longhair tomorrow."

140

He turned and disappeared.

In the tent anxious glances were exchanged. Then little Joe Fiore sprang to his feet. "I'd just as soon die making a break for it . . ." He started for the door of the tent, but Cecil Potts caught his arm.

"Don't be a fool, Joe! You wouldn't get fifty feet. It'll be dark in a little while. We'll try it then . . ."

"I don't like the idea of sitting here waiting for it," Fiore protested.

"You think any of us like it, Joe?" Potts cried. "I've been wanting to go home for ten years. I kept putting it off. I—I haven't been in England in nineteen years." He added bitterly, "You think I want to be buried here on your American prairie?"

O'Hara opened his hand and exposed a little double-barreled derringer. "When they searched me, they didn't find this. I've been saving it . . ."

Leach scrambled to his knees, reached for the weapon, but O'Hara, laughing harshly, tossed it to the ground in the center of the tent.

"You can draw lots for it!"

Dick Selby lunged forward. "This is my line . . ." he began and then Leach struck him savagely in the face. "You'll be the last to get it." He kicked the gun in the direction of Cecil Potts, who scooped it up.

"Two shots," he said. "One for . . ."

"No," said Molly Quade. "I'll take my chances with the rest of you."

"It's a pretty thin chance . . ."

"They keep the horse herd out back of here," O'Hara said. "There's a bunch of twelve and fourteen-year-old kids watching them . . ."

"Are they armed?" Leach asked quickly.

O'Hara shrugged. "What difference does it make? It's a matter of causing a diversion . . ." He stopped, his eyes narrowing.

Leach leaned forward. "How far is the herd?"

"Coupla hundred yards. Far enough. I was thinking . . ."

"Yes . . . ?"

O'Hara laughed harshly. "They'll be holding a big

powwow, out there in the middle. I was thinking . . ." He held his hand out to Potts. "Give me back that gun!"

Potts closed his hand over the little derringer. "What for?"

"The diversion, you stupid Englishman!"

Leach watched the big deserter narrowly. "How?"

"During the powwow. A man could walk right up and with two shots—"

"Sure," exclaimed Sergeant Potts. "You might put one bullet right through old Sitting Bull's head. That'd be a diversion, all right. But what'd happen to you?"

"What do you think?"

"The idea's all right," said Potts slowly. "Only—" he swallowed hard—"We'll draw for it."

"Not me," declared Dick Selby promptly. "I'll take my chances with the rest, but damned if I'll commit suicide."

Joe Fiore sneered at the gunfighter. "And you're the big bad two-gun man!" He turned. "I'll draw."

"You, Sam Quade?" O'Hara asked mockingly.

"Count me in," Quade replied dully.

O'Hara snorted. "I just wanted to see if you had it. You're out, Quade; you're too old."

The Indian with the headdress appeared once more silently in the doorway. His beady eyes flickered from one to the other of the prisoners, then settled on Dick Selby. "You, come!"

Selby's mouth fell open. "Wh-what for?"

"You, come!" thundered the Indian.

Selby scrambled to his feet, cowering in terror. "No," he whispered, then his voice rising. "No, no!"

Corporal Fiore rose behind the frightened gunman and gave him a violent shove that sent him through the door of the tent. Outside, a couple of Indians grabbed Selby.

Those inside the tent crowded to the open doorway and watched as Selby was dragged in the direction of the huge fire around which some hundreds of Indians had gathered.

"They're going to burn him!" Sam Quade cried hoarsely.

Molly Quade exclaimed poignantly and shrank back from the doorway.

Selby was swallowed up in the throng and for a moment the prisoners did not know what his fate was. Then, there was a great commotion among the Indians and they began to fan out, down the street between the two rows of tents.

O'Hara was the first to guess what was coming. "The gauntlet," he gasped. "They're going to make him run it."

"What's a gauntlet?" Potts asked uneasily.

"You'll see in a minute. Look—they're forming a double line. They start Selby at one end—he runs down the line . . ."

"What for?"

"For the fun of it," snapped O'Hara. "The Indians' fun. What do you think they've got all those clubs and tomahawks for?"

Potts recoiled in horror.

"Depends how fast he is," O'Hara went on. "He may not get ten feet. If he can run he'll miss a lot of them. He might get fifty feet . . ."

Outside the Indians were lining up. Aside from the shuffling of many feet and a grunt here and there along the line, the Indians had become strangely silent. Of Selby there was no sign. He was down at the far end of the line. Whether he knew his fate or not, those in the tent did not know.

"It's getting dark," Potts said suddenly. "Ten, fifteen minutes more . . ."

"They won't stop with Selby," O'Hara said evenly.

"No," Leach said heavily. "They picked him first because, well, I guess there's someone here from that village where we had the fight this morning."

A scream of awful terror split the early evening air. Selby had learned his fate. A roar went up and down the line of Indians. At the far end there was a commotion, yells and whoops—and then silence.

"He didn't get far," Leach said soberly.

"Here they come again," Sam Quade cried. "Wh-who'll it be?"

O'Hara whirled on Potts. "Give me that gun."

"What for?" Potts demanded.

"Your diversion, damn you. This is your chance . . . !"

The three Indians who had borne off Selby were march-

143

ing steadily toward the tent. Inside O'Hara smashed Potts in the face with his fist and tore the little derringer from his hand. He stuffed it into a pocket and then, whirling, leaped out into the open, just as the Indians came up.

"I'm next," O'Hara snarled at the savages.

The Indian who spoke English looked steadily at O'Hara, then shot a glance at the door of the tent. Then he raised his shoulders and let them fall.

"Come!" he said to O'Hara.

O'Hara walked off between the Indians.

"Damn him," swore Leach. "He's cheated me."

"John," sobbed Molly Quade, "is that all you can think of—*now* . . . ?"

"She's right, Leach," Cecil Potts said coldly. "O'Hara's a brave man . . . and we've no time to lose. Joe . . . Quade . . . !"

"Ready, Sergeant," chirped Joe Fiore. He got down on his hands and knees and scuttled to the rear wall of the skin tent. He raised it a few inches. "It's gettin' pretty dark, but I can make out the horse herd. Only—"

"What is it, man?" cried Potts.

"Indians," Fiore said softly. "A slew of 'em."

"O'Hara promised a diversion. But whether it comes or not, we've got to go." Potts turned. "Miss Quade . . ."

Molly started for the rear of the tent, stopped and looked at John Leach.

In that instant something snapped inside of Leach. Erased in one blinding flash was all the bitterness that had been in him for so long.

He said: "Molly . . . !"

A sob tore from Molly's throat. "John," she cried. "John . . . !"

He stepped toward her, took her in his arms—and then a spiteful crack came from the center of the Indian village.

"O'Hara's signal!" roared Potts. His mouth said something else, but the words were drowned by the sudden, hideous clamor that went up among the Indians.

Joe Fiore tore up the rear flap of the tent, held it up a foot or more. "Come on!"

144

"Hurry!" Potts added.

Leach thrust Molly ahead, helped her scuttle under the flap. He followed and outside the tent caught hold of Molly's hand. Behind him came Sam Quade, then Potts and Joe Fiore.

By the time the little corporal got through the others were already running swiftly toward the horse herd, a good two hundred yards away.

And off to the right, a hundred yards, Indians were running at breakneck speed toward the hub of the village.

Leach never let go of Molly's hand during that swift rush for the horses. Cecil Potts, unhampered, swept past him, but Molly and Leach kept ahead of Quade and Joe Fiore.

So it was Potts who met the first Indian by the herd. He was a boy of only thirteen or fourteen, but he had a carbine in his hands. He materialized out of the herd, saw Potts and the others coming at him and stopped in his tracks, frightened half out of his wits.

Only for an instant. He threw up the carbine, then. Potts was less than twenty feet from the boy, when the carbine went off. He broke in his stride, but his momentum carried him on to the boy. His arms flailed out and he carried the youth to the ground with him.

Leach hurdled over Potts and the Indian boy, let go of Molly Quade and caught the rope bridle dangling from the neck of a tough Indian pony. He jerked the horse forward, reached out for Molly, and with a single heave raised her onto the horse's back.

"Ride, Molly!" he shouted. "Ride . . . !"

He lunged for a second horse, missed it as it reared up, and headed for a third animal. He caught hold of a bridle and was jerked off his feet by the animal. He scrambled up, clinging to the bridle and pulling down the horse's head savagely, vaulted onto its back.

He slapped the horse's withers and using his knees forced it forward away from the herd. He caught a quick glimpse of Sam Quade mounting a pinto, then spied Fiore running toward an Indian, who was kneeling and aiming at Fiore.

The gun cracked and Fiore howled at the top of his

145

lungs: "Missed me, you goddam heathen!" He dove for the Indian youth and went down on top of him, smashing away with his fists.

That was the last Leach ever saw of him. He was riding now, following Molly Quade fifty feet ahead. She was skirting the pony herd, riding swiftly and surely. Behind Leach came Sam Quade.

And that was all. Potts and Fiore would not be riding.

Or Sam Morrison, alias Dennis O'Hara.

146

Twenty-three

THERE may have been pursuit; Leach didn't know. But the darkness fell so swiftly after they fled the Indian camp that the prairie was like the bottom of a well before they had gone more than a mile. The three fugitives, closed in by sound and slackening their speed, rode abreast. There was no conversation at all for almost an hour."

Then Leach spoke: "Let's stop a minute!"

Molly moved up beside him on her horse, as Leach dismounted.

"What are you doing, John?"

"I'm going to listen," Leach replied. He handed her the reins of his mount and, dropping to the ground, pressed his ear to the grass.

He listened for a long moment, then got to his feet. "All right."

Sam Quade spoke out of the darkness. "We're heading north."

"Yes," Leach replied. "Thirty miles north."

They rode on through the darkness, sparing their horses and twice skirting Indian villages at a safe distance. At the first Leach counted more than a hundred fires.

An hour before dawn, Leach called a halt. "We've traveled thirty miles, at least. There's no point in going on and this is as good a time as any to rest the horses."

He helped Molly from the saddle. "Sleep if you can," he instructed.

She shivered under his touch. "I'm tired, but I don't think I can sleep."

"Lie down, anyway."

"And you?"

"We don't dare turn loose the horses and we've no picket ropes . . ."

"I'll hold them," Sam Quade offered.

Leach hesitated, then surrendered the reins of his own horse and that of Molly. "I'll take over in an hour."

He dropped to the sod beside Molly Quade. For a moment he sat still, listening to her breathing. Then a hand touched his arm, slipped down to his hand. Leach's fingers closed over it.

"It'll be all right," he said.

"I know." She was silent for a moment. "Maybe I can sleep now."

She stretched herself out beside him, her hand still in his. Leach sat beside her thinking . . . thinking. . . .

He awakened with a start. Without realizing it he had dozed off, with his face on his knees. It was broad daylight, the sun already an hour above the horizon.

Beside him, Molly Quade slept peacefully on the short buffalo grass. The horses . . .

Leach sprang to his feet. There were only two horses, a hundred feet away. And Sam Quade was nowhere in sight.

Leach started running for the horses. As he neared them, relief flooded through him; both horses were hobbled with short lengths of rope. They could graze, but could not run. There had evidently been a rope on Quade's horse.

Unhobbling the horses Leach led them back to where Molly was still sleeping. He looked down at her for a moment before speaking. Then he called: "Molly!"

Her eyes opened, were blank for a moment, then brightened. She sat up. "John!" Her eyes went past him. "Where's—Father?"

"I fell asleep," Leach said. "Just woke up a minute ago. These horses were hobbled—"

"He's gone!"

He nodded.

"Where?"

"I don't know . . . I—I'm sorry."

"He was . . . afraid of you." She could not keep bitterness from her tone.

He made no reply. Last night . . . last night was gone.

He held out his hand to help her mount, but she

148

ignored it and threw herself upon the back of the little pony. She took the reins from him without touching his hand and sat on the pony, waiting for him to lead the way.

He mounted stiffly, turned his horse to the east. "We'll have to try it blind for awhile. If the Indians were right, Custer is ten or fifteen miles east of here, maybe a little south." He frowned. "But O'Hara said thirty miles from camp. Those Indians who brought in the news had to travel thirty miles. They probably sighted him around noon, a little before. He wouldn't stop before night." He shook his head. "In that case he'll be west . . ."

He turned his horse and kneed it. It started off at a swift lope and Leach had to hold it in to allow Molly to come up. They covered two or three miles without speaking, then Leach, worried, turned south. After a mile or so, he halted.

"I don't see any dust down this way," he said.

"I've been thinking," Molly said slowly. "Maybe we should split. You go one way and I—the other."

"No," Leach said promptly. "We'll make a circle. We're bound to cut their trail, or see dust. Seven hundred horses will raise a pretty big cloud."

Molly lapsed into silence and rode beside Leach as he turned eastward. They trotted along for two or three miles, then began gradually heading north. Ten minutes in this direction and Leach exclaimed:

"Dust!" He pointed to the north.

He sent his horse into a swift lope and in another half mile the dust cloud ahead became more distinct . . . and wider.

"They're moving west," he announced. "We'll try to cut them off."

The dust cloud grew slowly, for it was a clear day and visibility was good. An hour passed, two. The dust cloud was still moving westward, broken a couple of times as the column passed behind hills.

The sun was high in the skies, when Leach and Molly finally climbed a high knoll and looked down into a broad valley. Now at last they saw the source of the dust cloud. A long column of cavalry, five or six miles away.

149

"That's it!" Leach cried.

Molly exclaimed, "We've got to catch them. That village O'Hara told about . . ."

"I know," Leach said. "It can't be so many miles to the west." He did not call attention to the long cloud of dust that had materialized on the southern horizon.

They put their horses into a gallop, down the long incline into the broad valley. The mounts were none too fresh but they ran well enough for two or three miles. Then Molly's began to fall behind.

Leach pulled up. "Three minutes' rest," he called. She stopped her horse, smiled wanly at him.

"You think I haven't seen the dust to the south."

He inhaled deeply. "I guess that's caused by the warriors from the camp we left last night."

"I know. There's going to be a battle . . ."

". . . The worst these plains have ever seen!"

"We'll be in it?"

"I wish you could avoid it, but—well, I think your chances are just as good with the regiment, as alone on the prairie. Indians will be everywhere in a few hours."

"John," she said, "I've been thinking . . . it's—it's going to be all right. I—I understand about Father . . ."

Across the prairie came the rattle of gunfire. It was faint, but continuous.

"Come on!" Leach cried.

And now they drove their horses to the last bit of their tough endurance. The animals fairly flew across the buffalo grass. Ahead of them, the column had disappeared into a small patch of woods, but Leach had marked it and headed straight for it.

A mile. Both his and Molly's horse were laboring, but Leach, leading the way, was unsparing of his mount. He dug his knees into its sturdy ribs, raked the flanks with his heels.

They tore into the trees, burst through and saw dismounted cavalrymen ahead. A crackling of rifle fire came from the head of the troop, but there was more firing, distant firing off to the right and ahead.

Leach's mount stumbled, but made a quick recovery and plunged on. A soldier saw them, rode toward them.

150

It was a man from Troop M of the Seventh. "Sergeant Leach!" he cried in astonishment.

"Where's the captain?"

The man pointed and Leach raked his horse's flanks. But it was no use; the animal was utterly spent. Leach sprang to the ground, shot a quick look back and saw Molly dismounting, then ran forward.

Lieutenant Gregson materialized out of a troop of soldiers.

"Leach, by all that's holy . . . !"

Panting, Leach pulled up and saluted smartly. "Reporting for duty, sir. There are four thousand Indian lodges at the Little Big Horn and—"

"It's true, then!" cried Lieutenant Gregson.

"You know?"

"Sam Quade caught up with us an hour ago. The former sutler at Fort Lincoln . . ."

"He's here?"

Gregson shook his head. "Major Reno's in command here. The general split the column a couple of hours ago. He—he went north . . . toward the Little Big Horn."

"He'll be ambushed there!"

"He already has been. I—I only hope the sutler got to him in time."

"Quade went after General Custer?"

Gregson nodded. "Here—here's Captain Holterman and—Major Reno."

Leach snapped to attention and saluted the two officers. Captain Holterman regarded Leach sternly. "Where have you come from, Sergeant?"

Lieutenant Gregson saluted the captain. "He's just verified Sam Quade's story, Captain Holterman—about the lodges at the Little Big Horn."

Major Reno groaned. "Then it's all up with Custer."

"We'll have to join him," Holterman said promptly.

Major Reno shook his head. "We've got enough on our hands here. There are more Indians ahead of us here than I realized."

"And three thousand coming up from the south, sir," Leach said.

Major Reno turned on his heel, started running. "Bugler!" he called. "Sound the retreat."

Captain Holterman started to follow the major, then turned and pointed at Leach. "Sergeant, assemble the troop!"

Leach saluted. "Yes, sir!"

Molly Quade ran up, caught Leach's arm. "I'm with you, John . . . to the end!"

Twenty-four

IT was a retreat, but it could have been a rout. Only the great peril of being alone in the area teeming with Indians kept the troops together. Major Reno, commanding, was in front of the column that headed for the ford by which the battalion had crossed earlier that afternoon. The Sioux gave way for the column but harassed the sides and lashed the rear.

The three troops of the Seventh fought the Indians at their deadliest efficiency. The agile ponies of the redmen dashed headlong at troopers when their guns were empty. When troopers fired at them the Indians were suddenly on the far side of their mounts. Indians died, yes, but so did troopers and there were many, many times more Indians than soldiers.

When an Indian died there were a dozen to replace him; when a trooper fell, the command was weakened by an important man.

That Molly Quade was somewhere with M Troop, Leach knew, but he did not catch even a glimpse of her during the entire two-mile flight to the river. He was himself at the very rear of the column, where he tried, with the few soldiers that were not too frightened, to stem the ever-attacking Sioux. Men went down; if they were merely wounded—well, that was too bad. There was no time to pick them up. An able-bodied man could not be sacrificed for a wounded one.

At the front of the detachment, the pressure of the Sioux forced the battalion away from the ford, so that the soldiers hit the raging flood of the stream that was full. It was a narrow river, fortunately not more than twenty-five or thirty feet wide at this point, but the banks were high on the side of the soldiers and appalling on the far side. But Major Reno plunged his horse into the water and his soldiers followed.

Sioux rose up on the far, high bank and poured a withering fire upon the soldiers in the water. Horses were struck, began thrashing, and soon the water was a seething, churning maelstrom. Pressure from the rear forced the soldiers ahead.

And, then, as the troopers reached the far side, a gash was seen in the high bank. To the soldiers it was a miracle; they charged their exhausted horses up the incline and at the top fought Indians hand to hand. The latter retreated to shooting distance and Major Reno formed his men upon the high plateau. A semblance of order was created and troopers began to cover the river passage of the middle and rear of the column.

The Indians did not follow across the water, but rode downstream to the ford and crossed over so that soon a semicircle of them ringed the remnants of the battalion at the edge of the precipice that hung over the river.

But scarcely had the last man crossed the river than a cheer went up. Through a curtain of dust came blue-clad troopers. Harassed by Sioux the men came fighting every step of the way.

It was Captain Benteen's battalion, sent off in another direction early that afternoon. They, too, had been attacked by overwhelming forces, but the coolness of the veteran Benteen had saved many lives and the battalion was stronger than Major Reno's. The combined force numbered at this time over four hundred men, but there were easily twenty times that number of Indians opposed to them and the combined force dug in for a siege.

The newcomers shared ammunition with Reno's force and, under Benteen's orders, began digging rifle pits. By nightfall, the remnants of the two commands were in fair condition. They were protected from the direct fire of the Indians and only a unified charge could decimate them. And for that, the Indians apparently had no stomach. They harassed the besieged through the night, but by morning the pressure of Indians was not so strong.

Indian riders came and told of General Terry, riding up through the valley of the Big Horn. There were Gatling guns with the general.

Rain fell in the morning and helped the besieged. They

were still ringed by thousands of Sioux who crept gradually closer to the semicircle and made occasional charges, but the respect of the Indians for entrenched cavalrymen was great and the charges were too cautiously made.

At noon the firing diminished but a new danger threatened. The Sioux had fired the grass and a cloud of smoke soon enveloped the beleaguered soldiers. The edges of the fire were beaten out by the soldiers and through the smoke the Seventh saw a column of Sioux—marching off! Terry was too close.

But Terry camped in the valley that night, himself in a state of siege. The Seventh remained on the plateau overlooking the river. Except for pickets, the men slept that night and in the morning the valley was clear of Indians. A troop, sent out by Major Reno, made contact with General Terry and the fate of Custer was then learned. The General was dead and so was every man who had been with him.

The Seventh returned to Fort Abraham Lincoln, at Bismarck. Lieutenant Gregson was the sole surviving officer of M Troop, for Captain Holterman had remained in the valley of the Little Big Horn. Less than twenty enlisted men finally filed back into the barracks they had occupied during the winter.

Leach's position was clarified, then. Lieutenant Gregson came to him in the orderly room, where Leach had gone for lack of any other place to bunk.

"We're in the same position we were after Nelson's Island," he told Leach. "Only this time the captain won't be returning to take command." He paused. "I've been told that I'm to retain the command, but I have no lieutenants. Oh, I suppose I'll get some eventually, but I want one now, so I've put you down for the special officer's examinations . . ."

"The Lieutenant," Leach said, soberly, "seems to forget that I was posted as a deserter. . . ."

"Who posted you?" Gregson asked. "Lieutenant Brown was ordered out of Deadwood, the day after you left yourself. There was no time for paper work."

"Nevertheless . . ."

"Nevertheless, my eye!" exclaimed Gregson. "The detachment moved out to join the troop, which in turn joined the regiment. The regiment fought in the Big Horn. You were there and I know *how* you fought. As a matter of fact, I wrote two paragraphs about you in my report. . . ." He held out his hand to Leach. "I expect to be the best man at the wedding."

"Wedding?"

"She's visiting with my wife now," Gregson said, "but she can't visit forever, can she? And now that her father's dead, she can't live at the fort. Unless she marries an officer."

"How long?" Leach asked. "How long before I can take that officer's examination?"

"You've just taken it," chuckled Gregson. "And you passed. Congratulations—Lieutenant!"